ADVANCE 1

"*Mother Tongue* is not only dramatic and engrossing, it is also insightful and wise. Read it! Read it! You will never forget it!"

—Jane Smiley, Pulitzer Prize-winning novelist and author of *Perestroika in Paris (2020)*

"*Mother Tongue* is a gripping and gorgeously written novel of identity, loss, and redemption."

—Hilma Wolitzer, author of *Today a Woman Went Mad in the Supermarket*

"A beautiful, wise, spellbinding novel that dramatizes, in the most lucid prose, a woman's pursuit of her own lost identity."

—Joanna Scott, author of *The Maniken* and *Careers for Women*

"The "what-if" question that triggered this novel evokes a nightmare scenario: What if I found out I was kidnapped when I was a baby? In beautifully precise prose that resonates like the best poetry, Kornblatt's central character Nella/Naomi, the kidnap victim and a writer of fiction herself, discovers and creates her own lost story and the lost lives of all those linked to her."

—Wayne Karlin, author of *A Wolf by the Ear*

"In Joyce Kornblatt's exquisitely written novel, *Mother Tongue*, a middle-aged woman discovers her long-lost identity along with the layers of loss spiraling from her having been kidnapped at birth. The immediate and long-felt impacts of this tragic loss—crossing generations and continents—are explored with compassion, precision, and depth. Sympathetic characters, an abundance of human wisdom, and beautiful, lyrical prose, combine to make *Mother Tongue* a wonderful read."

—Elizabeth Poliner, author of *As Close to Us as Breathing*

"*Mother Tongue* is a tender and sensitive story about family secrets, loss and recovery from loss; a wise and lyrical meditation on the nature of love."

—Gail Jones, author of *Our Shadows (2020)*

"What a fully immersive reading experience! The writing is hypnotic, the story strange and irresistible, the insights into the human condition occasionally breathtaking."

—Monica Wood, author of *When We Were the Kennedys*, *The One-in-a-Million Boy*, and *Ernie's Ark*

"*Mother Tongue* is a beautiful, arresting novel. The clarities, prisms, temperaments, and tenacious obsessions are transfixing. If one question every novel asks is, "how does one define existence?" then *Mother Tongue's* difficult answer is that what keeps us together and what keeps us apart is made tangible by both reality and perception."

—David Biespiel, author of *A Place of Exodus* and *The Education of a Young Poet*

"Lucid, humane, and gorgeously written. In a slim novel with a big vision, Joyce Kornblatt sets her scarred but hopeful characters free to discover that loss is the *mother tongue* of us all — and that rupture contains the possibility of wholeness."

—Rona Maynard, Author of *My Mother's Daughter*

MOTHER TONGUE

A novel by Joyce Kornblatt

This North American First Edition

Cover design by William Oleszczuk

Trade Paperback ISBN: 978-1-7350273-1-9
Ebook ISBN: 978-1-7350273-2-6

Publerati donates a portion of all sales to help spread literacy. Please learn more at the Publerati website.

For my mother, Shirley Nathanson Reiser

Mother Tongue

A novel by Joyce Kornblatt

“The wait is long, my dream of you does not end.”

— Nuala O’Faolain, *My Dream of You*

“Rethinking one’s past is a constant responsibility.”

— Iris Murdoch

“. . . from the beginning of time, / in childhood, I thought / that pain meant / I was not loved. / It meant I loved.”

— Louise Gluck

Nella

1

My name is Nella Pine and this is my life's story, as new to me as it will be to you who reads it here for the first time.

I am the secret and the one who whispers the secret into your ear.

I am the crime and the narrator-sleuth.

I came upon the facts of my existence as one who returns to her home in the midst of a burglary: here is the shattered glass, the rifled drawers, the thief with the booty still cradled in her guilty arms.

When I was three days old, a nurse named Ruth Miller stole me from the obstetrics ward in Mercy Hospital and raised me as her own. This was May 7, 1968, in Pittsburgh, Pennsylvania. In Paris, ten thousand students rioted in the streets. Martin Luther King had been dead for a month, and Robert Kennedy's killer struck in June. The war in Vietnam was at its peak. In the midst of these larger convulsions, a smaller one – deadly as napalm, precise as an assassin's bullet – in the form of a nurse who kidnapped a child and vanished from sight. I was a healthy infant, with a head of dark hair and an iodine stain shaped like a butterfly in the center of my brow. During the futile search for me and my abductor, that marking would become famous for a while, *the butterfly baby* featured on news reports and front pages and missing children flyers in post offices and community centers and supermarkets all over America. By the time the authorities abandoned their hunt, the iodine stain had faded away, my most distinguishing characteristic no longer there to identify me. And as often happens to babies born with a full head of hair, that too was gone. I looked so little like the photo snapped of me in the hours following my birth that Ruth herself could begin to believe that I was a different infant entirely, not the one she'd taken from a mother in Room 32B who slept through the deed in sedated post-partum oblivion.

At the end of her shift, Ruth lifted me from my crib in the newborn nursery, settled me into a sling she wore beneath her raincoat, and walked out undetected into the balmy Pittsburgh dusk. Smoke from the steel mills still turned the air rancid then, and yielded sunsets of exquisite and memorable radiance. If I had not been stolen away, if I had been able to witness again and again the evening sky of my birthplace, I would have learned early the lesson I am struggling now to accept: beauty resides in blight, and blight in beauty – each holds the other like a seed in its hand.

We traveled by taxi to the airport. Ruth retrieved the suitcase and diaper bag from the locker room where she'd stowed them the day before. In the Ladies Rest Room, she fed me a bottle, changed me, dressed me in a flowered fleece gown and matching knit cap large enough to pull down over the stain she'd already doctored with pancake make-up, the kind models use to achieve the look of false perfection.

Ruth herself exchanged her nurse's uniform for a gray pleated skirt, a pink blouse with a Peter Pan collar, and a gray cardigan – a uniform of sorts of the conventional woman, though of course she was anything but. Did she touch up her own make-up, there in the mirror over the sink, in view of other passengers about to leave Pittsburgh for unknown parts? Did somebody notice how pretty Ruth was – her shiny short black hair, her solemn green eyes, her mouth upturned slightly in what always seemed like a subtle smile even when she was sad or angry or embarking on a terrible crime? Did somebody notice, and smile back into the mirror, one reflection acknowledging another, reversal greeting reversal, a little wink as if to say: *Nothing is as it seems?*

In the suitcase, a passport bearing her new identity: Eve Gilbert, her late father's first name taken as her last, and *Eve* a promise of paradise, of course, new beginnings, and signifying darkness, too, a shadowland where one can hide, hide out, hide away and from, vanish from Time itself.

And a false birth certificate, which recorded my fabricated father whom she called *Philip*. Her own alias. The one she invented for me: *Nella*, which I now see resembles *null*, the condition of non-existence. And the notary's raised stamp, which even a blind person could verify by touch, nothing but a fraud.

Nella.

Nothing.

Nulla.

Nil.

Nella Gilbert: to learn that this was not my name was as much a shock to me as the one I would have suffered if I had discovered that the body I inhabit was not my own, my reflection in the mirror nothing but a sham, a canny deceit, an optical illusion I had mistaken for the reliable truth.

In the airport, I slept peacefully against my kidnapper's heart. Soon we would board a flight to Los Angeles, transferring there to Honolulu, then on to Sydney, my abduction carried out and completed in thirty-six fateful hours.

And if her confession, forty years later, left me knowing less than before she admitted her deed, if questions rattled my sleep like spilled coins from a purloined purse, what could I do but investigate further?

Beyond the meagre field of facts, I moved on to other kinds of evidence: memory's stuttering tongue, imagination's hieroglyphs. In my thickening file, a record of dreams detailed as fingerprints, omens complex as DNA, lies in which the truth rests furled like a snail in its decoy of armoring shell.

In other words, I followed every lead.

This is my account of that investigation. Some might call this document a fiction, and to you I say: Yes, if by fiction you mean the truth a fevered soul yields up out of its alchemical heat.

We are meant to burn.

We are meant to tremble, quake, call out from our sweat-drenched beds in the singular voice that emerges, like a new language, from our suffering sleep.

My refugee students have been trying to teach me this for decades. They've come to instruct me from all over the world, migrants whose mother-tongues seem to have spoiled in their mouths, fluency turned into sour garble, sweet familiar speech now bitter in an English-speaking land. When I learned the secret of my birth, I might as well have been flung onto a smuggler's fishing boat for a night journey over foreign seas. I might as well have sold all my possessions for a one-way ticket on a cut-rate airline, destination *away, elsewhere, anywhere, far.*

I am setting this down in September 2013. I am forty-five years old. I make my living teaching refugees how to speak and write English. In the process, I hope I help them reclaim the voice they often lose when they leave their native language behind, in the choices they make to save their lives and the lives of their families. I myself write stories, inspired often by the courage of my students to leave a record, to bear witness, to remember and imagine. I have published many, in literary magazines, here and in New Zealand, and gathered them together in books via a good small Australian press. I have set aside a novel-in-progress for this narrative instead. *My name is Nella Pine and this is my life's story, as new to me as it will be to anyone who reads it here for the first time.*

Ruth/Eve planned her crime for months.

She did not conceive of it as a crime.

With the authority of prophecy, of divine revelation, a dream arrived one night and never left. She surrendered her life to it. She ceded to it the power she gave to the orders doctors at the hospital inscribed on the charts of her newborn patients. A nurse is trained in obedience. The dream commanded her to choose an infant in her charge and create a life with it as if the bond between them were the natural one of birth. Though not religious, the woman I would come to believe was my mother was obedient, and the voice of the dream became the oracle on whose word the dreamer founded her new life's faith.

Psychosis.

Or a devious alibi not a soul could contradict.

Both explanations compel me. I see their logic. When I consider madness as her motive – my entire identity based on a slow chemical leak in Ruth Miller's brain, or a sudden electrical storm that one night erased forever the map of reason from that tissued labyrinth– then I can grieve for her as well as myself and the family from whom I was taken. We can all rest together in the ruins of Ruth Miller's delusion, kindred refugees fleeing the same disaster.

But what if she invented the story of the dream solely to shield herself from judgment? Perhaps she produced that lie as a container for the others, a nest in which all her fabrications seemed to have hatched organically and without blame. Perhaps no dream at all arrived as the onset of an obsession which snatched her reason from her exactly as she had lifted me from that hospital bassinet.

Instead, she may have been sane and selfish, calculating, a woman who wanted a child and took one from someone else. Shoplifted me, as it were, and made up a cover story in case she were ever confronted with her crime.

Wouldn't I have to cast her out?

For a time, I did. For a year. After her death, and the discovery of her letter of confession to me, I hardened and numbed. Clenched heart, fisted soul, body rigid, and the mind furled shut. Better to soften to the pain, I have learned, than to die in such contraction. *Rigor mortis* before the fact. What seems to be a bed of nails is just the earth, in the end. Every person's pallet, not just mine. The same breath breathes us all.

As the plane traveled through each time zone, Ruth/Eve jettisoned more of her past, the life she had lived as Ruth Miller falling away like baggage released into the atmosphere. As if she were on a jet that could somehow yield up that cargo without a loss of pressure that would down the flight itself. But at such an altitude, the air is so cold that anything entering it would immediately freeze, every blouse and shoe, wool jacket, lace slip, every pair of nylon stockings, all her undergarments, each flannel nightgown, every dress and hat and skirt perfectly preserved in their space-borne containers. That is how I imagine her memories: filled suitcases orbiting the planet, a history neither destroyed nor claimed. Although she must have believed that she was rushing toward a new life in Australia, it actually was the past toward which she was bound, that jettisoned baggage waiting, like so many asteroids, to plummet at last straight through the roof of her house.

We arrived in a night storm. It was as if the plane were landing underwater, that was how dense the downpour was. Below us, Sydney's lights were starfish, electric eels, schools of iridescent minnows. The landing wheels dropped like rafts to hold us steady on the uprushing sea. Then, the seeming water turned to tarmac as the wheels made their magic contact. *Magic* because that was Eve Gilbert's language now, the story into which she had descended, a fairy-tale strange as flying animals and wizard wands and beauties – a woman and an infant – awakened to themselves in a foreign land. That she had entered the trance rather than escaped it did not reveal itself to Eve for decades. It was impending death that woke her to her life at last, the horror of her act finally clear to her, the wish to *make things right,* as she wrote me in her letter of confession, profound and impossible.

Can you piece together a shattered glass?

Zen masters teach: *This glass is already broken.*

I'll choose that hard solace over blame and bitter remorse.

Our lives are already broken, birth a shower of shards beyond the gestures of ordinary repair. Give up the glue of habit; it won't hold. To be wholly broken: that's Eve's bequest to me.

Broken wholly.

Holy broken.

Broken whole.

Words shift shape, in kaleidoscopic flux. How not a life's story, then, that house of words which is our shelter and our storm?

2

In our rented room, Eve made a bed for me in a bureau drawer.

We lived in Balmain, before it was the favored Sydney address it has now become. I live there now, in a sandstone bungalow a few blocks from the boarding house where my Australian history began. We stayed there for a month. The rooming house we occupied then sold last week for more than a million dollars; the rear windows look out on the old Colgate factory, a once-vacant industrial hulk renovated into trendy flats.

In 1968 Balmain was mostly an enclave of run-down three-story terraces, some turned into flats or boarding-houses for stevedores and factory workers; bungalows tiny as bed-sitters; rows of fibro-sided semis; and the shops of Darling Street named for their immigrant proprietors who lived upstairs: Papadopoulos Fruits and Vegetables, McLean's Bakery, Fazio's Shoe Repair. On Saturdays, the outdoor market stalls opened and pushcart vendors claimed their spots in the churchyard, transformed to the bazaar that still flourishes today. Hawkers sang out their offerings, bargainers yelled down the prices, children begged for ice cream while their mothers picked over produce trucked in from Hunter Valley farms and their fathers stood in line, trading cricket scores while they waited for a sausage on a stick: from a distance, Eve might have mistaken Balmain for New York's Lower East Side or Boston's Roxbury or Pittsburgh's Hill District just after the Second World War.

Except that the jacaranda tree in the middle of the churchyard dropped its petals like a fall of lilac snow.

Except that rainbow lorikeets and magpies and fierce-eyed currawongs choired in the boughs.

Except that the tongue of the Balmain shoppers was English, in its particular Australian drawl – my mother's American accent would always mark her as foreign, and I would grow up mimicking her diction as much as that of my peers, my hybrid speech intimating to me the lost life I would wait forty years to discover, as if Eve were storing the truth like a family heirloom kept in a vault, to be passed on to me only upon her death.

Which, indeed, she was.

From the window in our rented room, a sliver of blue water drew Eve's eye. Beyond the prison-like factory compound, this glimpse of the bay. In Pittsburgh, too, she'd learned to squint just so until the solid masses of steel mills blurred, as if they'd melted from the heat within, and the city's three rivers shifted into foreground, glittering ribbons of light it seemed the smokestacks could not dim.

The eye is hungry for such light.

It doesn't see killer-microbes weaving like ruin under the water's skin. It doesn't see families of fish scrambling for poisoned food.

Every day she walked down the narrow lane to the ferry dock and sat on a wooden bench. Freighters collected the Colgate goods there, and deposited cargo for the plant, so it wasn't a peaceful harborside spot.

Eve was oblivious to the noisy commerce. She was fixed on sea and sky and the baby sleeping in her arms. Sydney is always a city at one's back, the luminous harbor and its vast mirroring heaven drawing the gaze away from the made world to the elemental one.

In that month she must have spent a hundred hours studying the water and the clouds. It didn't rain again that May. It was a warm autumn. Each day opened up to Eve a kind of monastic order: feed and change the baby; dress; buy a cinnamon bun and coffee and piece of fruit at the corner coffee shop; walk two blocks to the bench beyond the ferry stop; spend the baby's morning nap-time there, then return to the boarding house with a take-away salad sandwich and bottle of milk; feed Nella, change her, eat lunch, lay the daughter in her drawer and the mother in her bed, where afternoon dreams arrived like letters from another world.

Letters addressed to *Ruth Miller,* dated decades before, messages from childhood delivered to a Sydney address. They consoled her, these archaic narratives. She should have been having chase dreams, her pursuers right on her heels; there should have been arrests and trials and leg irons and prison cells. That would have made sense, the repressed terrors of capture finding form in daily nightmare visitations.

Instead, she dreamed of picnics with her parents in Pittsburgh's Schenley Park, when her father was still alive and her mother knew her name. Dreamed of trolley trips with her classmates to the indoor gardens of Phipps Conservatory, orchids and lilies and bleeding heart (here the imagery dips into nightmare possibility, a hint of her crime encoded in those tiny crimson petals). The perfume of those dream-blossoms remained with her even after she woke, as if our rented Balmain room were filled with the flowers of girlhood innocence.

And what did *I* dream?

What images could *I* bring with me from my previous life?

I mean my Pittsburgh life, those three days following my birth. I mean the nine months *in utero* I floated in the dark belly of the woman who read poetry to me and spoke to me in French (I pretend) and played Mozart's *Magic Flute* on the hi-fi she and her husband bought to celebrate my conception.

Not that I have any such knowledge: I'm as capable as Eve was of inventing the life I need and inhabiting it like a squatter laying claim to someone else's home.

For a while, in a conversation with myself, I stole the details from a story I recently heard about a couple who chose to carry to term the five-month-old fetus they learned was afflicted with a rare genetic disorder: as soon as the baby was born, the doctors said, she would die, her lungs unable to function, air a poison to her for whom the amniotic fluid was the only element in which she could survive. The parents chose to carry her to term, startling even themselves with their decision. They would give their daughter the only life it was possible for her to have. They gave her a name: Fleur. For the next four months, they read poetry to her, they spoke to her in French, they played Mozart's *Magic Flute* for her. Fleur was born at home and died an hour later, peacefully, her parents crooning her name to her as she drifted away.

That baby's story isn't mine.

Mine starts at the end, moves backward to the third day of my life, then springs forward again like a boomerang, a truncated narrative arc in which the true beginning lies beyond the teller's reach.

Or so I have believed.

Sometime last year, after receiving my mother's letter, I went to see a psychic healer in Kangaroo Valley.

I am not the kind of person who goes to *psychic healers*.

I go to the dentist for annual cleanings and the doctor for flu shots and the optometrist for eye exams. But a friend insisted I needed to visit this woman whose intuitive gifts would show me a path out of the wilderness in which I now seemed to be lost. I couldn't eat, I hardly slept, I'd taken sick leave from my teaching work. A few months before, seeing a psychic would have been the last thing I would have done. But that morning I made the drive from Sydney, and in just over an hour, I had passed from warm ocean breezes to the crisp air of the Southern Highlands, the rolling pastoral landscape a swatch of green England or Southern France set down in a desert continent ten thousand miles away.

I found her house by Braille: the mist showed me only the reflections of my headlights against two illumined circles of road. As if driving into a dream, reliable markers vanished, and a new map created itself out of air. Serena opened her door. Her image remains vivid: a corona of shoulder-length permed auburn hair, silver hoop earrings, layers of velvet and cotton and silk, embroidered Chinese slippers. Her face was kind, I remember that. I never knew her surname, or if I did I have forgotten it.

I sat on a velvet love-seat and Serena faced me on a carved wooden chair. She assured me that I could recall, in detail, my conception, my uterine phase, my birth and the parents who welcomed me into their arms. In the healer's lounge room, through a wall of windows overlooking the bush, the morning mist was so thick on the ground that it looked as if the houses across the road were rooftops floating in air. I myself felt as if I were floating somewhere about the love-seat, watching myself listen to the healer. The work would be hard, Serena said, and the sessions might be experienced as assaults on my rational mind, trance states revelatory and exhausting. She explained this all with the same matter-of-fact tone a doctor uses to describe upcoming surgery and its aftermath, or a course of chemotherapy whose side-effects are as violent as the symptoms of disease. Something like convulsions might arise, Serena said; fevers and pain were not uncommon; temporarily I could lose the power of speech. *I suggest you come on Fridays,* she said, *to give yourself the weekend to rest.*

I never saw Serena again.

Months later, fever and pain shook my bones for hours one night, and left me mute for days. *Temporarily you could lose the power of speech.* Faces hovered, disembodied, just below the ceiling; I memorized features and form, an archaeologist cataloguing anatomical details of newly discovered mummified remains. Was it memory itself that had offered up these images to me, the tomb I excavated no other than my own living mind? Within days, the faces blurred and disappeared, as if a dig site had collapsed and tons of silt fell again on what had been retrieved. What remained was my conviction that those faces had come to me as a kind of knowledge I would never have countenanced, would have dismissed as hallucination or superstition or chicanery passed off as fact. I still carry their images with me, tucked away, the way a child secretes a stick of gum in her pocket, for later.

Now it is *fact* that arouses my suspicions. Eve has turned everything I believed on its head. What of those declarative sentences I used to revere, their incisive assurance, the way they bear down on a single truth with absolute end-stop clarity? My students chanted such sentences as if they were liturgy: *This is my street. My house is blue. I live in Sydney.* They yield their authority now to the interrogative. Fish-hook question marks on which I hang, one after another, the facts I took to be *my life.*

Your parents are Paul and Deborah Gordon, and they named you Naomi, which I changed to Nella after I took you away.

Gordon, like *gordian,* the impenetrable knot.

I have become an etymologist, Eve, every word you left me turned into a puzzle of origins.

A woman named Ruth and a child named Naomi. The Biblical bond scrambled, loyalties inverted and subverted, no son/husband there as bridge between the two females, and the younger one kidnapped, no *Whither-thou-goest-I-will-go* choice at all.

Yet perhaps Ruth Miller believed my birth-name was a sign on the map her mind was constructing and receiving at once, a message from guides to whom she listened with a fanatic's faith. Perhaps Ruth recognized exactly the same biblical suggestiveness in that name that I am writing about here. Perhaps it blazed before her like a burning bush, and the name we left behind on the hospital bassinet was the sole reason she took me rather than another, Paul and Deborah Gordon unwittingly signaling Ruth by their choice of *Naomi* instead of *Melissa, Susan, Caroline.*

How my fate might have changed if the bracelet on my wrist had carried one of *those* names instead.

Or is this line of conjecture my own invention?

Maybe she took me for my hazel eyes, or the pleasing shape of my head. Maybe she flipped a coin or consulted the I Ching yarrow sticks she kept beside her bed in an embroidered silk bag or asked the tarot cards for advice on which infant she should abduct.

Allow me these dead ends.

No Thru Road, the sign would say in Australia.

I have been so starved for explanations. I've chased down clues like a police dog sniffing the subtlest aroma of contraband, or bodies buried in shallow graves, or half-starved children praying for rescue in wilderness shacks days after they've stumbled away from the family camp site.

I am forty-five, it is 2013, the century has turned, the rescue team has long disbanded, the wilderness into which I vanished is an island continent ten thousand miles from my native land. I never prayed for a search party to find me, of course. I never knew I was lost. I was an Australian child serenaded to sleep by mynahs in the palm trees outside my window and bathed each morning in the gum tree's minty perfume.

If there is rescuing to be done, then I am the search party and the one who will be found. This story traverses the world, but the resolution is interior. The compass aims inward. The needle points to the heart.

3

That time in the boarding house was Eve's pregnancy, I see now. Nine months compressed to one in which the embryonic Nella became Eve's daughter as surely as if I'd grown in her womb. As if she'd been sent far away from home, unwed and shamed by the baby she was not meant to conceive. Except she would not give me up, she would not consent to losing what she most wanted in the world. She would embrace her exile as her salvation, transform a fugitive's flight into an immigrant's brave and steady journey in a chosen land.

The funds she'd saved were running out, and, three weeks after our arrival, my mother had to find a job. In the *Sydney Morning Herald* she saw an ad for a full-time placement in a nursing home in Narooma, a fishing village on the ocean five hours south of Sydney. She'd read about Narooma in a travel guide – *Touring New South Wales* – that she'd found in the top bureau drawer in our room, along with a Bible and a slim volume by Mary Baker Eddy on Christian Science faith-healing.

Narooma suited Eve. She liked the idea of a small town into which we could more fully disappear, the kind of place where one can live inconspicuously, where fears of surveillance and even capture vanish into the fiction of an unchallenged newly crafted identity. Small-town people were trusting and good-natured, Eve believed. Welcoming to a widowed mother come to put a tragic loss behind her – the husband dead in an accident whose details she couldn't bear to share, not even with their child, which would keep her from having to invent them. When neighbors would ask her, gently, how she came to have traveled so far, to the other side of the world, her eyes would glisten with tears and she would answer, *Philip died.*

No one probed beyond that simple sorrowful declaration. The nursing home liked her letter of application and her American training and didn't bother contacting the hospital references my mother said she would provide, though she knew if they were asked for, she would have to pretend the job was no longer needed. They hired her after a cordial ten-minute phone interview, my mother standing in the boarding-house hallway talking into the shared telephone on the landing, and the next day we rode the bus down the coast to our new home.

In a hinged double frame, kept on the upright piano in our Narooma lounge room, photographs of her parents, whose real names she divulged to me in her letter of confession: Gilbert and Sophie Miller, those names, too, contrivances, but officially so. Names replacing the ones they'd lost at Ellis Island, 1937, on the eve of Europe's conflagration. Jewish names difficult for the immigration clerks to understand, strange names better to change. They were Americans now, after all, wasn't that the case? I had grown up knowing those photographic images as William and Lucy Gilbert, yet another layer of falsity that even in death my grandparents were forced to wear.

Child of those who had lost everyone, my mother wreaked catastrophe again, taking me from parents left to flounder in the pain of those whose losses are incalculable, unspeakable, beyond the capacity of memory to revive or repair.

I was compelled, she wrote. *I was compelled.*

4

Narooma means *clear blue water,* named by the Yuin people who have lived there for 40,000 years. The village is almost an island, surrounded on three sides by the Wagona River, its estuary and the Pacific. Just beyond the shore a real island – Montague: famous for its lighthouse, its penguin colony, and the migratory seabirds who come there to breed and rest during their endless cycles of flight and return. Whales visit every year, on the way to Antarctica. The Yuins know the island as Barunguba, the eldest son of Gulaga Mountain, who moved away from his mother, but not so far that she couldn't watch over him, making sure her child did not come to harm.

Eve and I arrived forty-five years ago. We were like the spores of non-native plants brought into Australia on the shoes of foreign settlers, seedlings taking root in a terrain for which we were not intended, into an ecology our very presence disrupted. Invaders as surely as if we were part of a conquering colonial force.

Or perhaps we were meant to arrive exactly when we did. Perhaps we came like the seabirds who know in their cells when it is time to move from one place to another. Did Ruth/Eve follow a route inscribed in her from birth? *I was compelled.* That implies that I, too, was destined to be kidnapped from my natural parents and brought to Australia, abduction the means by which life moved me organically to my intended home. Did the anguish of my parents serve some larger purpose we don't yet have the science to understand?

I can't abide such superstitions.

I can't abide a scenario which suggests that Paul and Deborah Gordon were meant to wake one morning in Pittsburgh to their newborn's empty hospital bassinet and the heart-crushing blow of their loss that would come for them for the rest of their lives in the middle of the night, or arrive like a jolt of electricity in the shower, or force them to pull off the road and weep, or turn around for home en route to a dinner party, knowing that the pain which had flared could take hours to subside and social conversation would be unendurable in the midst of such an attack. I can't countenance a worldview which suggests they had something to learn, lessons to master. That losing me was exactly what their souls had ordered. As if they'd sat around a ghostly table before their births and planned out their meeting and my arrival and then my disappearance. A play called *Catastrophe* in which I was the main character who vanishes after the opening scene. Whose absence haunts the narrative, precludes denouement, renders closure impossible, defies the yearning for catharsis and redemption.

I refuse to believe they were born for *that* plot.

And yet the alternatives – caprice, accident, chaos, malevolence – are equally hard for me to embrace. The truth is that I don't know why I was stolen or why the Gordons had to suffer so or what Ruth/Eve imagined she was finishing or starting when she kidnapped me.

I only have a story I have woven from filaments pure and intangible as light. I only have what we all do: a dream I call *my life*.

Water-bounded though Narooma is, from my bedroom window I didn't see water at all. I looked over our back garden to a paddock of browned grass, and in the distance beyond that, to green Gulaga Mountain, a great volcanic relic that spent its fire forty million years ago and collapsed into itself. Giant craggy cliffs softened into undulations, earthen mounds that appear and vanish in morning mist. Gulaga seemed at times like an apparition rising out of my dreams, rather than a dependable geological formation, solid and verifiable.

Much as I have come to think of myself, I see. An apparition, neither solid nor verifiable.

It is, I have come to understand, a relief to acknowledge the truth.

I am writing this account in that room, looking out of that same childhood window, into the shimmering light in which everything definitive dissolves.

In my girlhood I didn't know the mountain as Gulaga. I knew it as Mount Dromedary, which is what Captain Cook named it on January 22, 1770. It was the first thing he named on his journey to Australia, and the naming was a theft. A name is meant to confer honor and meaning, but the name a thief gives to the stolen place or person is a lie from which disorder arises each time the lie is uttered. As if the true name waits for release within the false one. Rattles the cage, as it were. Cries out.

Nella looked out of her bedroom window at the green contours of Mt. Dromedary, and Naomi gazed at Gulaga.

Eve hung the washing under Mt. Dromedary's shadow, and Ruth saw the mist rise from Gulaga's body.

This narrative is my naming ceremony, and hers as well. I can't reclaim my truth if I leave hers behind. Our stories are intertwined like strands of DNA.

Today I read a news story about Natasha Kampusch, the young woman abducted years ago as a child in Austria and held in a dungeon bedroom a neighborhood away from her mother's home. She is suffering, the psychologists say, from a version of the Stockholm Syndrome, in which one who is hostage begins to identify with and feel empathy for the kidnapper. Hers flung himself under a train when he realized she'd escaped. *I am going through a certain kind of mourning*, his victim says.

As am I, Ruth/Eve. As am I.

5

Questions:

If I'd sat down to write a record of my girlhood before I knew about my kidnapping, would it be the same narrative I write now?

Would my memories alter?

Why?

Aren't they preserved like relics inside amber – insects, feathers, flower petals, leaves, pebbles, moss, and lichen, just as they were millions of years ago?

Can't I write about my girlhood free of the pressure of knowledge that has come to me since Eve's death?

Or has she stolen from me a second past – the one I lived with her erased along with the one I would have lived with the Gordons?

I refuse to grant her that second theft.

If I am not to be stolen again, lifted out of memory as surely as I was lifted out of the hospital bassinet and carried against her body from Pittsburgh to Sydney, then I cannot relinquish the truth of my love for her. Inside that love, a real life grew, *my* life, imprinting itself in tissue, blood and bone.

The scent of wisteria and lilac on the route from home to school each Narooma spring, how I liked to close my eyes and follow that perfume like a blind tracker.

The *baby pancakes* she made me on Sunday mornings, each medallion plump with berries we picked on walks in the bush.

Those walks through gumtree, stringy-bark, melaleuca forest and swamp, where we learned together a landscape as foreign to Eve as it was brand new to me. She carried a little pocket-sized notebook and wrote down the foliage she recognized from the copy of *Native*

Australian Landscape she studied at home. She learned wildflowers – *waratah, banksia, rock orchid* – and birdcalls – *sulphur-crested cockatoos, galahs, kookaburras* – and rock formations – *chert, turbidite, pillow lava* – the same way, and taught them all to me on our expeditions of my early childhood. I'd often come home with a few treasures in my pocket: pine-cones, stones, fossils, seed pods, fallen blossoms, feathers. When they started falling off the overcrowded window-sills in my room, I'd place the day's gathering on a bookcase Eve bought for me at the markets one day – raw wood she painted blue, my name stenciled on the side in gold: *Nella*. By the time I was seven, the shelves were filled, not with books but with relics that carried with them a narrative of our walks and the history of the bush from which these objects came. It was a way I assembled a past. I have all these early findings in a wooden chest I bought at twenty, when I was moving out on my own.

Even then, dedicated to collecting the clues.

*

Picnic suppers on the jetty, dolphins performing their dances at low tide, the sky going red and purple and gold, Eve and the other parents murmuring together in that adult conversation that sounds to a child like a tender chant in the background, an invocation I hear to this day: *safe, safe, safe*.

Nostalgic? Perhaps. Nostalgia organizes itself around the beautiful and the good and flattens out pain that spiked and smouldered. I know this. My girlhood had its pain, like everyone else's. Of course: this is not meant to be a document of denial. It is simply that it would be easy to efface all that nourished me, to pretend I wasn't happy and secure as much as I suffered. Of course I suffered, as did Eve. Human beings suffer. But she was my mother and I was her daughter and I don't remember wishing even once that it wasn't so.

Only after I learned that it wasn't so, did I wish that, but there is no way to undo love.

Things fell into her lap. The woman who hired Eve on the phone had a newly widowed neighbor, Olivia Stroud, looking for someone to share her house with her. Eve called her from the Balmain rooming house. Olivia said, *You and your baby sound just like what I need, you come here straightaway from the station,* and gave my mother the address: 2 Tamarind Road. Moreover, Olivia offered to *mind the baby while you're at work,* and when Eve asked how much that would cost, Olivia Stroud said, *I'm the one should be paying you, seeing how it will be just the medicine I need.*

She's a good baby, Eve said, as if Olivia needed convincing.

And so it was that before I was two months old, yet another pair of arms reached out to claim me, a third woman held me to her as if I were the greatest treasure life had ever bestowed. Would I have known in my cells the violent theft which resulted in this maternal trinity, or did I simply receive the love each offered as a bounty of nurturance? Both stories are true: I carry in my body the wound of my abduction, and the salve to the wound. *Beauty in blight, blight in beauty: each holds the other in its hand like a seed.*

From the bus station, a taxi shepherded us to Tamarind Road, and the plain brick bungalow on the corner. It was winter now and a cold southerly churned the seawater to foam, fishing boats came in early, eucalypts bent toward the rain-battered ground. Yet you would have found Narooma beautiful that day, as Eve did, the vivid colors of sun-drenched days paled now to a subtle palette. Sea, sky, and earth all shades of taupe and gray, so muted it was hard to tell where one part of the landscape ended and the next began. Eve was always glad for cloudy days. They reminded her of Pittsburgh, I imagine, as if the northern hemisphere wasn't a world away.

Mum, I asked her once, *why don't we go and visit where you're from, in America?*

I thought of it as her birthplace, not my own. Without a single photograph to evoke for me the place of my conception and gestation and birth, without keepsakes, the notion that I'd begun my life *over there* was an abstraction, at best.

They're all gone, she said, meaning her parents and my fictitious father. Meaning other relations never named or recalled. *I don't want to be reminded. I'm better off here.*

She looked at me with grief both given and withheld: *Here is my sorrow. Don't make me feel it.*

Whenever I brought up Pittsburgh, she would stop breathing for a time, as if even an exhalation might threaten her resolve. Her body would go so stiff that I'd want to reach out and test that she was alive, though such a gesture would have violated the borders of her silence. I studied her for a sign: eye-blink, mouth twitch, a finger's tremble. I doubt I knew how frightened I was by her utter stillness. I doubt she knew how fully she hardened, how it alarmed me, how I scrutinized her for proof I hadn't gone too far. Turned her to stone and unable to call her back. All of this happened under the surface of our otherwise happy dailiness, as if water had frozen in reverse, from the inside, while here above the ice, the warm flow of ordinary life remained.

And thus I learned at a young age not to probe my mother for any information about the past. Her annulment of the life we'd fled became my own; what she erased I also gave up. It was what was required of me to protect the one family bond I had, the bond between the two of us. Sometimes my yearning arose for knowledge of an ancestral history, for a web of relationships in which I was held like others, a weave of aunties and cousins and grandparents and uncles and yes, the father dead, I believed, before my birth. At night in my bed I'd invent a family with whom one day I'd reunite. I imagined relatives knocking on the door and announcing themselves to me: *I'm your cousin Lila, and I've traveled all the way from California to find you* or *You don't know me, but I'm your Uncle Bill on your father's side.*

Eve wasn't like the refugees I would come to teach, whose houses and neighborhoods became replicas of the countries they'd fled, kitchens fragrant with the smells of foreign spices and stereos playing all day long the music of forsaken homes. Eve wanted to expunge the land she'd left behind, though the United States insisted itself into Australia at every turn. I was her accomplice before I knew there was a crime.

Narooma, though, was freer than Sydney from the intruding fashions of America, and it was easier there to forget, or pretend to forget, the texture of that earlier life. Olivia didn't even have a television – *I like the radio better,* she said. *You can move around and do your chores while you're listening.* – so we were spared all the American sitcom re-runs that Australians love to this day. And now I see how fortunate that was for Eve, the usual screen of American images that flickered for hours a day in most Australian homes absent from ours, and she free of incessant reminders, prods, claims on the heart that might have broken through her impenetrable disguise. Only in her dreams would my mother's origins arise again as clearly as if she were back in girlhood; but memories would have been welcome in that private somnolent realm. It was in conversation that they threatened to reveal too much, to spill over from what was admissible to what would be damning, cherished stories turned to incriminating evidence, precious vignettes transformed to exhibits A and B and C.

Looking back, I can see how adept she was at maintaining the fiction of who she was and who she had become. A narrative consistency maintained at every turn.

Life as an alibi.

For a criminal, there's no reprieve from deceit: each moment compounds the crime, lie supports lie, falsity yields falsity, an intricate construction of appearances we name *myself.*

Aren't we all implicated, as if we are all felons of a sort? Who *is* exempt from masquerade? We are all hiding, camouflaged, as if survival itself depends on façade. Who gives up the disguise willingly and turns herself in? *I am a fraud,* we yearn to confess but cannot.

Psychologists say we resist the truth even when we're paying to unearth it. We dissemble even when we vow we're not.

Of course, the taxi driver could not have known he was bringing a criminal to her hide-out. He could not have known I was *the butterfly baby,* robbed from her parents weeks before on the other side of the world. He would have talked with Eve about the weather, most likely. Cloudy and cold. Maybe he mentioned that his grandson was coming down from Sydney soon *for a little fishing with his Pops.* And Eve would have said something like *That's so nice for you both.* Was there a flicker then in her guarded heart of the sorrow in which my real family was drowning, or a memory of her own grandparents whom she had never known? Or was she already walled off from her own griefs and terrors, so that she truly believed she was having an ordinary conversation in a taxi headed for Tamarind Road?

I can see Olivia watching for us through the window as the taxi slows in front of the single-story three-bedroom brick veneer house, and she is there on the front landing when Eve and I emerge from the cab. In the small front yard, a stone river winds through a native garden. She greets us with both hands waving, as if we were long-lost relatives returning for a reunion, rather than strangers she has never seen before in her life. Who could resist such a welcome? For a moment Eve imagines Olivia is family, perhaps a great-aunt or a second cousin, and she feels the relief of a homecoming that has no basis in fact.

Perhaps rescue is always return. That she was on the run does not counter the sense that she has arrived at a safe harbor. The simple house could have been a palace, that is how great her good fortune seems. Eve would return the wave if she weren't carrying me in one arm and fumbling in her shoulder bag with the other for money to pay the driver. *Hello, hello.* In that way our new life commences – a fare paid, a greeting received, a short walk down a stone path. The door opens and we enter.

6

Until I was five years old, and off to school, Olivia cared for me during the weekdays, while Eve was at work. Olivia was plumped by age – she was past sixty when we came to live with her – and had cultivated the common habit of eating as a cure for loneliness. In her cardigan pocket, I could always find something sweet: plastic sandwich bags filled with lollies or chocolate drops or licorice strips. She wore her long gray hair in a braided ponytail, which gave her the look of an ageing amiable child. Her thrift-store clothes were some young Bohemian woman's lacy camisoles, gypsy skirts, stenciled T-shirts. Her sad eyes were free of bitterness, as if the losses of her life had worn her down like burnished wood, without warping her. Some young playfulness remained intact, and my presence called it forth. We took delight in each other.

As I grew from infant to toddler to child, I preferred Olivia's company to any of the children on the block. They must have thought me shy, reclusive, one of those little girls who hides away in her room with books and paper dolls and a make-believe companion she talks to all day in an invented language only she and the pretend-friend understand. It wasn't like that at all. Olivia was such an inventive and energetic playmate. Why would I leave her in favor of the Peterson sisters or Eddie Malone or the Lawson brood on the corner? Olivia turned her housework into games that included me: when I held two corners of sheet to be folded, we pretended it was a magic carpet; when she swept the rugs, we talked to the vacuum cleaner as if it were a friendly animal named Hoover come to eat up all the dirt in our house. Every moment was game, theatre, invention.

One of my first memories is Olivia's voice, its particular timbre and timing, a kind of ongoing music to which I woke up and which also sent me off to sleep. Her voice a medium in which I lived, along with air and the water in my bath. Bathed in her talking. Inhaling her words. As I got older, the sounds organized themselves into a language I was learning from my life with her, and what she said registered itself on me as *her story*.

That reminds me, she'd begin, and a memory would begin to form itself as speech. All through my girlhood, Olivia told me her life in fragments, vignettes, half-scenes slight as the spoonfuls of honey I learned to suck clean when I had a sore throat. Story, too, a kind of honey, sweet and curative, especially given the paucity of Eve's shared memories, her past a mute zone, it seemed, out of which she had emerged into this languaged Australian life. From Olivia, I learned about the possibilities of a past that lived in its telling.

She'd lived her whole life in Narooma, the decades stacked neatly and congruently on top of each other like layers of New South Wales sandstone. Infancy, childhood, girlhood, marriage, widowhood – each strata self-contained and yet clearly related to the next. This continuity consoled her, and me, even though the content of her stories was often bleak. Convict ancestors, alcoholic father, depressed mother – *a drinker,* Olivia said, and *sad,* the straight-forward daughter not given to the specialized dictions of psychology or theology or politics. Then the childless marriage – *our lot* – and her husband's heart attack two months after retiring from his schoolteacher's job. *His time came. Nobody gets to choose.* It was from Olivia that I learned a model of reconstructing the past that I would teach to my migrant students, and to which I am trying to turn myself, displaced person that I too have become. Life as a house you can re-build after each disaster. Sitting here in my childhood bedroom, I am writing my way back into a story from which Eve's confession evicted me, though her intention had been to deed to me the truth.

Or was it herself she was taking home?

Leaving me, as it were, homeless.

The mind, I am discovering, is more ocean than land, more liquid foam rather than geological stratification, a formless movement rather than a solid mappable terrain. All language gestures toward the depths of that ongoing flow. Thoughts toss before us like seaweed the ocean waves throw up and reclaim – a word, an image, a memory, a phrase. Here, and then gone. Even a whole idea beaches itself on the page. Then a person gets up to make a meal or walk the dog or leave for a job in the city. The body's life calls us back to itself. What we read disappears into the waters of the unconscious. We can do a little fishing but see if anything stays caught. The mind is a dream of those transient uprisings.

Yet still I fish.

On a Zen retreat, weeping to the teacher that I now had no idea who I was, she reminded me of the Buddha's words: *O house-builder, you are seen. You will not build this house again.*

That house of words, that is our shelter and our storm.

Olivia was slow in school, so the teachers said, but years later she discovered the joy of reading books, having stayed away from them for decades, she said, as emblems of her girlhood shame, and her library card became, in adulthood, her most prized possession. She'd never lacked friends, she was cheerful in a way that suggested a genuine appreciation for being alive rather than some sort of false uplift meant to keep qualities she said she must have inherited from relatives generations back, *before all our troubles started*, forgiving in one short inclusive phrase her parents and teachers and anyone else who'd caused her pain.

I always like the music in church, she told me, and hummed hymns whose melodies seemed, still, to uplift her, though she seldom went to services. *I got less sure about God*, she explained, and then her special wink: *Hopefully God still has faith in me.*

Troubles and cheer, doubt and faith: I learned from Olivia that contradictions asked for acceptance, that it is fruitless to yearn for a single-stranded clarity in a world of braided truths, each thread wrapped around its opposite.

A double helix in every breath.

No doubt there is another Olivia I never knew, one whom people found odd, and stubborn, and too wrapped up in me for my own good. *Acts like she's the mother,* they might have said, or *How's Nella going to learn to be with other children if Olivia keeps her all to herself like she does?*

And likely gossip snagged her as it does everyone in a small town where people live all their lives. But I never learned what those rumors might have been, what secrets of hers, true and otherwise, lay in the town's memory knotted up with everyone else's, and anyone could pull a strand from that tangled nest whenever they wanted, twist it, taste it even, show it around and then put it back for another time.

In the evenings, and on weekends, Eve devoted herself to me and Olivia receded.

I knew myself against each of their bodies.

Olivia fleshy and warm, a terrain of yielding sand dunes into which I could sink, a landscape that adapted itself to my presence.

Eve angular, cool and solid as a tree against which I could lean or clamber, knowing its form would never bend.

Each offered a particular and precious kind of comfort, though I do know that at the end of each week-day afternoon, my ears pricked up like a dog's at the sound of Eve's footsteps on the gravel walk, and in those moments of transition I released myself from Olivia before she officially transferred me to my mother's care. Though I didn't wail or protest when Eve left for work in the mornings, I do remember a trough of sadness I had to cross alone, inside, on the way to Olivia's good-hearted guardianship. Back and forth I went, from one woman to the other, baby and toddler and young girl held and created in that fluid exchange.

Did memories of my actual mother thread through my dreams, or arise as unease or teary spells or a kind of fogginess that might have been interpreted as *drifting off*? I believe every child has moments of psychic disturbance, a sense of a larger field in which she can't locate what it is, exactly, that summons her attention.

A distant music, a faraway light, a mysterious breeze that prickles the skin.

Did Deborah Gordon call to me from beyond the conscious dailiness of my Narooma life? *Naomi, Naomi, Naomi.* Perhaps the sound of my real name rippled the air in the lounge room or flashed across the verandah like electrical lightning or brushed past my ear like a buzzing fly as Olivia took me to the playground. I might have turned or jerked or felt a sudden itch. I might have become sleepy or spit out the food I'd just been fed. *Naomi.*

Did she call?

When I found Eve's letter of confession, all of it shocked me except for one thing: my name. As if I had heard it in the background all my life. An imprint, awakened.

Naomi.

She called.

7

You must wonder how a woman who erased her past could have much of a presence in the years that remained. You might imagine such a woman as withdrawn, unavailable, enigmatic and aloof – all of this a strategy to avoid detection. An underground life lived in shadows and silence. The town hermit. The neighborhood recluse. The village itinerant who always seems to be passing through, even after decades at the same address.

Eve managed to avoid this fate. Of course, there was the moat she built around my questions, or the curiosity of others, but it was so easily accounted for by her widow's grief that everyone, including me, was willing to allow her this island of isolation. It seemed respectful to protect her mourning, and then it became natural to think of her as *a very private person,* as she liked to describe herself. If you didn't ask Eve about the past, if she knew she was safe from the pain of such probing, if she could trust the permission to re-invent herself from scratch, then she did just that, with bravura.

That's the word that comes to mind – *bravura* – though she was in no way flamboyant. Because of course it was a performance, every moment of her Australian life. She was never not on stage, never out of role, never simply herself. To be so would be to invite a moment of lapse on her part. An utterance that could be her undoing. An unbidden confession, in which she would have been ensnared in her own words.

When I try to imagine how it was for her to construct each day around a lie, I can feel in my own body what she must have experienced in her own. The mobilization of tension in the muscles and bones. The vigilant sensitivity in the spine, so that the back can never relax, the sensors there always on heightened alert for ambush from the rear. A tightness in the belly that makes it hard to the touch. The breath a bit too shallow. The eyes a bit too alert.

Here is Eve getting ready for work at Pelican Cove Nursing Home. The alarm goes off at 5 a.m., to give her time to wash, dress, have breakfast, wake me up and leave before her 7 a.m. shift. She takes showers, never a bath. She lays her clothing out the night before, and eats before she dresses, so that her uniform stays clean: a glass of orange juice, a cup of English Breakfast tea, one boiled egg and two slices of wholegrain toast with jam. In time, she develops a taste for Vegemite. When I am a baby, she feeds me, too: a bottle of formula at first, and in later months a bowl of rice cereal and mashed banana thinned with warm milk. Soon she's boiling eggs for both of us and toasting extra bread. As I get older – two, three, four, and then the years going to school – I am still sleeping when she enters my room to say goodbye. Her morning hug always feels like the end of a dream I am having, rather than a daytime embrace. As if she were lifting me from a lake in which I'd floated all night, and just as my head surfaces and I see the sky, she's gone. She closes the door as softly as she can – Olivia, too, is not yet awake, or if she is, she waits until my mother has left, so that the two of us can have that first-light contact alone. I came to know early that when Eve vanished, Olivia appeared, so I didn't suffer the anxiety many babies and toddlers do when their mothers leave them. Perhaps I already bore the imprint of Eve lifting me from the hospital crib not long after my mother Deborah had cradled me in her arms. Perhaps my theft eased my way even as it wounded me.

Eve wears the uniform Pelican Cove issued her when she arrived: a blue cotton short-sleeved blouse under a pinafore, blue-and-white-striped, and white oxford shoes. She has a cap for her head as well but doesn't put that on until she gets to the nursing home, anchoring it with two bobby pins she always carries in her pinafore pocket. Just above her heart, a badge that announces her name: Eve Gilbert, in printed black block letters. Official and factual, erasing questions before they arise. To Eve, too, the badge is convincing: *This is who I am.* She'll check it more than once in a day, I imagine, just to see the name reflected to her, keeping her clear about the life it announces.

Pelican Cove sits back from the main street of Narooma. The traffic passes by – tourists, truckers, interstate buses, locals on errands – and the residents in the nursing home hear the motored hum. But behind the bank of shrubs that hides the traffic from the deep front lawn and the circular delivery driveway, not a vehicle is visible, and those inside can often forget about the world of transport and momentum of which they used to be a part. Eve understands such forgetting well. It is how Pittsburgh is for her now, increasingly remote and lacking in detail. She rarely thinks about Ruth Miller during the day, and she almost never, now, replays the moment she lifted Naomi Gordon from her hospital crib and walked out of Mercy with a baby under her coat. Only in her dreams does her old life arise in vivid sensation and particularity, and then it is her innocent girlhood, not the woman's life defined now by a crime. When she was fleeing, and had a layover in California, she caught a glimpse of the newspaper there in which the infant's photo stared from the page and the word *Abducted* in huge letters beneath the image. For a moment, I imagine, at the gate waiting for the plane to Hawaii, she had misgivings and thought of turning herself in at the Travelers Aid desk. When the clerk asked her what she needed, she would say, *I need to be forgiven*, and then she would hand the baby to the stranger. But the impulse passed, the woman at the United Airlines desk announced that the plane was ready for boarding, and Eve felt herself and Nella carried forward, toward Australia. Sometimes she wishes Australians spoke a language other than English, so she could distance herself even further from Ruth Miller's life, from any memory of that moment when she might have turned back. If anything can be said to haunt my mother, it is that instant of remorse so fierce she nearly changed her course.

She punches in the code that gains her entry into Pelican Cove. The doors open and lock shut behind her. *Like a prison*, she has reflected more than once, but without the fear you might expect. She knows she will never be arrested, tried or convicted. She doesn't know how she knows, but she does. The observation could be made by anyone – you, or me – and the fact that she is a felon hasn't consciously troubled her since the day she boarded the plane in Los Angeles and headed off as Eve Gilbert, whose newborn baby nestled in the crook of her arm.

Yet, how much it must have cost her to hide from everyone who she really was. And how much she must have wondered if that reality holds much authority. Because she still felt like herself inside, Ruth arose a hundred times a day in Eve, that early uncontrived girl still peering through the eyes of the sham woman. She must have wondered again and again who she really was. Mustn't she have? Was she tormented? Was she frightened? Did she wish sometimes, ever, once, that she *would* be caught, a sentence passed after a quick trial, the deception over and done with at last? Or did she imagine she was living in a dream from which she would surely awaken, at home with her parents in Pittsburgh, their European past the only family nightmare she could imagine having to bear?

I am not so different. Am I Nella or Naomi? Am I the curious child Eve and Olivia raised, or the dreamy teenager, or the young hopeful wife I became when I married Alex Pine? Am I the woman whose marriage fell apart like a beautiful glass bowl dropped on the footpath, the shards scattered in all directions and the mending impossible? Am I the person writing these words, who looks for her real self and finds each identity she might have claimed in earlier years, or even a moment ago, ungraspable now, a kind of mirage in which no substance can be found?

Terror or freedom, what is this dizzy space in which I float?

8

I own the house on Tamarind Road.

Olivia left it to Eve and Eve left it to me. I inherited the family home, which I've reclaimed from the tenant to whom I rented it these past years, furnished until my return from Sydney this month.

The family home.

For a time, after Eve's death, I could only say those words with a bitter rue, if I said them at all. I tried to cut my ties to this place. I called the realtor in town and told her to put the house on the market. I phoned her back an hour later. *Not now*, I said, and knew I meant *Never*.

Inherited. Reclaimed. Return.

Olivia's natives still flourish in the small front garden. A poem of plants: banksia, ferns, grevillea, wattle, hibiscus, waratahs, kangaroo tails and brome grass, with a pebble path running like a river through the specimens. She liked eucalyptus mulch, and every spring a truck would deliver a mound of the fragrant shredded bark which I helped her shovel into a wheelbarrow and spread by hand. Eve and I kept up the garden after Olivia died, and the tenant who lived here in the years since Eve's death got a rent reduction for tending to the yard. The wattle blazed yellow when I returned, the bank of grevillea offered up their tender white flowers, and the banksia's spiky orange blooms covered the tall shrubs which bore them. In one corner of the garden, near the house, the crimson heads of the stand of waratah are just beginning to open now, the little florets on each blossom like dozens of secrets about to be revealed. Ferns border the driveway – after Olivia planted them, I'd watched for months as their young tendrils strengthened and spread, what had been barren dirt now a bank of deep green fronds.

The family home.

I've turned the dining room table into my desk, so I look out the bay window at the garden as I write. When I was a girl, this is often where I did my homework, and later my stories began to accumulate in lined exercise books I kept in a cardboard box under my bed. Eve had ordered some uniforms which arrived in the box from Work Wear Limited, and I covered the printed top with flowered shelf paper. Inside the front cover of each notebook, I'd write: *If found, please return to Nella Gilbert at 4476 9125. Thank you very much.* Eve would grow agitated when I announced my decision to be a writer *when I grow up.*

Do it as hobby, Nella, but make sure you have a proper job. When I resisted and said I thought writing was proper, thank you, she'd say, *I mean a job with a paycheck, Nella.* Her voice grew a bit shrill and agitated, as if I had poised myself on the top of a dangerous ridge. I thought her concern was for my welfare, and no doubt it was, to a degree. A single mother raising a child alone: she would worry that I, too, be able to support myself as she did via her nursing at Pelican Cove.

But now I understand that she must have feared, too, a writer's probing errands: to delve for the truth, to decode the clues, to burrow into the hidden and disguised.

I have asked myself if Olivia knew anything about Eve's crime. Not that I imagine Eve confessed to Olivia what she had done. But perhaps my mother talked in her sleep. Perhaps there were slips of the tongue, contradictions, gestures that pointed away from the words being spoken toward another silenced truth. The human heart is a leaky vessel, and however much we try to contain our secrets, they spill out in tiny drops of unconscious disclosure. Freud built his entire theory and practice around such leakage. Olivia may not have read Freud, but she possessed that sensitive alertness to the counter-narrative that all children from troubled homes cultivate. I experienced that radar as empathy: how aware she was of the slightest sadness or agitation or fear in me, and knew how to meet it with a smile or a hug or a cup of hot chocolate with a marshmallow sailing on top like my own resurrected spirits. Wouldn't that same attunement have registered Eve's inevitable incongruities? And then what would Olivia have done with such observations? I imagine her collecting them like fragments of glass from a broken vase that show up in corners and under chairs and impaled like tiny knives in the carpet's pile. Slivers that would cause injury if they penetrated skin, best watched for, retrieved, and discarded. Collusion of a sort, but not with a narrative she could have discerned. Denial of a sort, but not of a lie whose truth she refused to know.

My husband Alex used to say that his own childhood was *one question after another I never asked. What were we going to do? Blow up the house with the truth?*

Our house did not blow up.

2 Tamarind Road has weathered death and deceit, wind and rain and flood and even a fire next door that gutted the Andrews home while they were in Bali, and never crossed the property line between their yard and ours. Just one blown ember might have set our house alight. It was windy and hot. I was fourteen years old. In the middle of a sweltering January night, in what I first thought was a dream, Eve was pulling me out of my bed, and, still in summer pajamas, out of the front door to the neighbor's garden across the street. I saw the flames spike from the Andrews's windows, and then up through the roof, which crumbled like a charred biscuit into the burning house. By the time we were on the other side of the road, fire engines were screaming toward us. Five firemen rushed into the conflagration, and one remained behind to cordon off our home along

with the burning one, *because you can't be sure,* he said, *you can never be too sure.* Everyone who lived on our block was outside in night-clothes, as if the whole street had been evacuated. Holding me against her, Eve shook as if she too might collapse in on herself, like the Andrews house, but I was strangely calm. *Dissociation*, I would learn in university, studying psychology books which would help me understand the migrant students to whom I taught English, their stories matter-of-fact recitations of the traumas they carried with them instead of possessions, which they'd left behind in burned-out cities and bombed villages and drought-ravaged refugee camps where a tin pot was a luxury, if there was anything to cook in it.

Years later Alex would say the spirits were watching over us, Eve and me, that night of the fire next door. *Why would you believe that, Alex?* I said. You're not religious at all.

He smiled. *Watching over you for me,* he said. He touched my hair. *For me.*

In this narrative, chronology's gone up in smoke.

The categories of *past, present* and *future* melt into each other the way the walls between the rooms of that burning house gave way. When the flames subsided, who could tell where the kitchen had been, or the lounge room, or the bedrooms at the back? It was one charred and tangled space. Mr. Andrews stood in the middle of the rubble and collected objects that had somehow survived the devastation. An iron skillet, a glass candy dish shaped like a swan, a sewing box in which Mrs. Andrews's spools of cotton thread lay like jewels, inexplicably unharmed. He rescued these treasures as if they were religious objects, precious with potent meaning, which of course they were. He would take them into the family's next life, however improbable it must have felt to him that day that a new life could be created.

Eve's letter rose like a lick of flame that engulfed me and every inch of 2 Tamarind Road, but here I am, writing at the dining room table, its sturdy carved legs like an elephant's whose memory remains quietly and bravely reliable. There is Olivia's oak hutch with the glass-fronted doors, the shelves filled with her crystal goblets she'd found at a thrift shop and installed behind the glass doors *for the fun of it,* she said. *Though I came to love them same as heirlooms, if I'd had any of those.*

Now you do, Olivia. *Heirlooms.* Now they are in my trust.

In Eve's bedroom, open the carved Chinese chest she bought at a garage sale, and you will find her uniforms, laundered and ironed and folded, waiting for her to begin a new work week at Pelican Cove. Wherever I turn in this house, the objects of our lives await me, here for me to gather up, as if for an altar.

I am making the ritual as I write.

9

Before we met Olivia, her husband, George, was up on a ladder, nailing down a gutter that had come loose in the overnight wind, when he had a fatal heart attack and plummeted to the garden below. A neighbor said George looked just like Icarus, whom she had seen in a painting, because George's arms lifted like wings as he fell.

Olivia didn't see it happen. She was in town, doing the grocery shopping, and by the time she got home an hour later, the ambulance had taken George to the hospital where he was pronounced dead and transferred to the mortuary, waiting for Olivia to claim his body. As soon as she approached the house and saw the ladder splayed out on top of the plants it was crushing, she knew something terrible had happened. Mrs. Andrews from next door was sitting on the bench by the front door, her hands clasped in her lap and her ankles crossed, as if she were in church, or at a somber school assembly after some sort of national tragedy. *Olivia,* she said, *I have some bad news,* and Olivia said, *Is it George? Is he dead?* Mrs. Andrews said, *Maybe the doctors can help him,* but she'd seen the medics shaking their heads as they'd lifted his body to the stretcher. Olivia felt the lack of conviction in her neighbor's hopeful words, and knew immediately that George was gone, as if he'd sent a message to her directly: *Yes, I'm dead. Imagine that.*

The house was paid off, and Olivia could get by on George's schoolteacher's pension – he had just received his first check, *like winning the lottery,* he'd said – and hers from the government – *for being old,* she said, *for having lived this long. Which is work, of course,* and then her wry grin. She did do work for pay herself, but not much of it, and her customers paid her in cash – she was a seamstress – with crisp notes passed from their hands to hers without receipts. She never thought of herself as having a business, or being self-employed. She was just keeping herself busy while she waited for children, and when it was clear there would be none, she was consoling herself *with a little something to do*. She would have adopted, but George was opposed. *Blood is blood,* he'd said, and she wondered what that made her, a girl he'd met one Saturday morning in the newsagency, where they were buying birthday cards for family members. He lived in the next town, Tilba Tilba, and was up in Narooma, visiting his grandmother. They were both nineteen. After they married, they would give each other a birthday card every year on their anniversary – a private joke, a tender acknowledgement, a commemoration.

They had never imagined they wouldn't have children of their own. It seemed they had been sentenced for a felony they couldn't name, punished without knowing their offense. They never accused the other, Olivia remembered, nor did they embark on medical tests to discover where the problem resided. They accepted fate and *got on with life*. Perhaps they didn't want to know which one of them was responsible for the inability to conceive, afraid the knowledge would turn one against the other, however subtly that blame might have sullied the good will of their life together. *We soldiered on*, I heard Olivia explain once to Eve. *We soldiered on.*

Did Paul and Deborah Gordon soldier on? I try to imagine how they might have gone forward, put the one proverbial foot in front of the other, day after day, year after year. Unlikely they bore my disappearance with Olivia's stoic grace, not knowing what they were mourning, asked to accept a loss that had no certainty to it. Was I dead or alive? Was I safe or suffering? Was I returning or not? Perhaps they crumbled under the weight of their sorrow, or they existed in a netherworld of numbness to their own pain like those people who put their hand in a fire and don't feel the burning and the fingers are lost. How did my parents endure my theft? I am writing my way toward that knowledge, this record I am creating a kind of map that leads me to the home from which I was stolen, and the hearts riven by the crime.

When Eve and I arrived in Narooma, we conferred on Olivia a reprieve she would never have thought possible. She was no longer the childless woman, the barren wife. It was if she had changed her identity as much as Eve had, stepped from one life into another as one might give away a worn coat and buy a new one with a sudden windfall. She became Eve's mother and my grandmother, though we never used those words in our home. Yet they stitched us together as surely as the hand-sewn French seams Olivia was famous for in the garments she made for her customers. The woman whose own clothes were thrift-shop bargains had a gift for fine tailoring.

Our lives are Russian dolls, identities inside identities.

Like any animal, the territory I knew as *home* grew each year. When we arrived, the room that would become mine was Olivia's sewing room, and I slept with Eve in the spare bedroom, where Olivia had already installed a crib that a neighbor's granddaughter had outgrown. A mobile of red and green origami birds circled above me. Later they were moved to the kitchen, where they wheel now in their ceaseless arc above the sink. I had taken the mobile down when the tenant lived here, but when I moved back in, the first thing I restored were my beautiful paper birds.

I first met Alex in Year 6, and then not again for fifteen years. We could be sure the first meeting was the Year 6 class outing to Montague Island; his uncle Nick, with whom Alex had just come to live for a time, was our naturalist guide for the afternoon, and eleven-year-old Alex his uncle's helper. Alex was enrolled in the Catholic school in town, not the public one where I went. *For the first week I was in Narooma, Nick didn't let me out of his sight,* Alex would tell me years later. We were in that early stage of a romance when the story of the other is the most riveting tale ever heard. Each detail mythic, touching, memorable. *Took me everywhere and slept me in the same room with him. Saving you from more trouble, he said. I complained plenty, but he was firm. That's why your mum sent you to me, he said. To keep you good.*

Sent him to Narooma for a year, from Sydney, where his teachers wrote on his school progress reports that *Alex needs to concentrate more* and *Alex has been late most mornings this term* and *Alex does not have respectful attitude toward the teacher in maths class, and is encouraging other students toward pranks and silliness.* The principal phoned one night to say that Alex had been caught trying to break into another student's locker. He heard his parents argue about *what should be done with him*, in his father's words, who wanted more discipline at home – rules and punishments and *no more babying. You spoil him, Thyra. You let him get away with too much.* When the call came that police had arrived at the school *because boys were vandalizing the playground,* and Alex had been caught pulling the seats off the see-saw, *they shipped me off to Narooma,* he said, where he'd loved going for holidays, so it didn't seem like much of a punishment, or what his mother called *a desperate measure*, Uncle Nick being *a damn cool bloke* who knew the natural environment *like a native*, Alex said.

When Alex and I met again, fifteen years later, he'd begun to map his genes the way his Uncle Nick mapped Montague: a consuming interest in what was hidden and camouflaged, so that as you walked the trails with Nick as a guide, a whole new island emerged beyond the one that appeared to be there. *Secret business*, as the Aboriginal people say. A special kind of transmission that cracks open the world of facts to reveal something alive and nourishing and waiting to be taken in as food. Or shows you where the poison is, and medicine as well.

On Montague Island, a colony of seals, twelve-thousand fairy penguins, acres of pelagic fish, whale pods, vast schools of dolphins. Birds everywhere, breeding: wedge-tailed shearwaters, sea eagles, kestrels, crested terns, silver gulls, a pair of peregrine falcons at the northern end. The volcanic rock vibrates with birth, the island is a nursery for babies incubated, hatched and delivered and weaned. Alex's Uncle Nick showed us where the mothers find the food for their young, stands of grasses – mat-rush, bracken, tussock – good habitats for insects and seeds. Kikuyu grass, brought to Montague from South Africa as food for the goats that fed fisherman stranded on the island, spreads via runners which trap and strangle nesting seals. Conservationists have been at work to eradicate kikuyu, but it is tenacious, as invaders are. Along the coastal rock, above the spray line, bright orange lichen spreads across the stones like the marmalade Olivia made, so delicious on buttered toast.

10

I have been making lists.

Games I Played. Foods I liked. Songs. Friends in Primary School. Teachers. Friends in High School. Boyfriends. Teachers. Holiday Customs. Illnesses and Allergies. Things I Overheard. Lies I Told. Lies Told to Me.

I am looking for oddities, things that don't jibe. But nothing points to the fissures that were always just under my feet: *When I was three days old, a nurse named Ruth Miller stole me from the obstetrics ward in Mercy Hospital and raised me as her own.*

Now the earth trembles unceasingly beneath 2 Tamarind Road. Now I know what I was oblivious to as a girl: the world was always just about to collapse, the life as I knew it was never more than a flimsy shelter which the next strong wind could blow to smithereens.

Broken whole. Wholly broken. I wanted Alex to surrender his rage and be held by his shattering, while I stood on the side, so reasonable and contained and seemingly intact. All along I was falling with him, the ground having given way even when I thought it was solid under my feet.

I thought he was the damaged one, but both of us, it turned out, had childhoods that looked pleasant and safe and turned out to be anything but.

I am the crime and narrator-sleuth.

After I learned that I had been abducted, I wanted to flee the facts Eve now insisted I know, her letter giving me as little choice about my destiny as she did that moment she lifted me from my hospital crib and hid me against her heart. But then I remembered how Alex had railed against the truth of his own origins, first rejecting any evidence that was presented to him and then claiming it with such ferocity, he could have strangled anything that entered that burning embrace.

11

Year 6 marked me twice: Alex and I met for the first time that day on Montague, and a month later, just at the start of summer holidays, Olivia died.

She had been ill, but not with anything we knew was fatal. First a cold, then bronchitis, then pneumonia which landed her in the hospital. The problem they found wasn't in her lung, though. It was in her heart. A tumor growing in the left atrium. *Cardiac sarcoma.*

I had never been in a hospital before. Not even to Casualty for an X-ray after a fall, or to have my tonsils out – that would be the following year. Eve took me to visit Olivia on the day the diagnosis came, so I was in the room when the doctor arrived with the scan results. He said we should leave, not being family, but Olivia insisted she wanted us there, and reached out her hand to me as if to demonstrate our relatedness. *This is not good news,* he said, and I felt something in me take a photo of the moment, as if I knew this would be one of my life's central memories, a recurring image imprinted forever now in my cells, and thrown up on the screen of dreams when I was least expecting it.

Eve took Olivia's other hand, and it was clear to the doctor that Olivia claimed us as kin as we did her. We were a phalanx, a united front, a family whose relatedness would not be refuted. When he said *cardiac sarcoma,* I heard Eve's gasp, and her shock passed from her body through Olivia's to mine. We were in a windowless room, but in my memory the available light darkened, as if a storm had moved in where the sun had been present. And I felt a heaviness descend, the air itself thickening. It reminded me of the fire, how breathing was hard for days afterward.

The tumor was advanced, the prognosis dire. A month, maybe two. Pain that opiates could lessen, a possible stroke. A hospice nurse could visit the house, if Olivia returned there. I felt we were on a conveyor belt, moved along from traumatic impact to information to logistical planning, with hardly a moment between stations. Eve said she would take unpaid leave from Pelican Cove and tend to Olivia herself for as long as she needed her care.

And Olivia said, *No, I think it wiser for me to move to Pelican Cove. It's always seemed like a resort to me, all those prepared meals and such. Why not splurge?*

The unexpected humor, even from Olivia, passed like a counter-current through our shocked bodies and a wave of laughter traveled from Eve to Olivia to me, and even included the sober doctor himself, until the room vibrated with hilarity, and it seemed we were celebrating something we were meant to mourn.

*

As it turned out, Olivia died in the hospital, three days after the diagnosis, before the move to the nursing home's palliative care wing could be arranged and carried out. It happened in the early afternoon, the feared stroke sudden and fatal. The other patients in the ward with her had no idea she had died – she did not make a sound. I was in school, Eve at work *just for a few hours*, she had decided, leaving Olivia's bedside when it seemed she was resting comfortably, having been moved out of Casualty to a regular ward *as a transition*, the doctor said, though he had been wrong about the nature of the next step.

Olivia's one surviving blood relation, Thomas, a cousin – *a tiny family that shrunk even more in the wash*, she'd joked – had planned to visit her the following week, coming up from Tasmania, where he had a shoe store in Hobart and said he'd bring her *some comfy slippers.* He would come for the funeral instead, and tell some funny stories about their shared childhood, and return to Hobart with her set of Blue Willow plates *for the wife,* he said when Eve offered them to him, though I could see from the way he took the box in which she'd packed them up that they meant something to him too, even if he was the kind of man who wouldn't show his feelings.

George's remaining family had all left Narooma years before: a brother gone to Perth, a sister to Auckland, cousins spread from Sydney to Los Angeles to one who wound up in Reykjavik, Iceland, and sent photos each year while George was alive of the active volcano, Hekla, as if to remind us that the planet was still exploding, that nothing was stable, that the coldest country on earth was fed by fire. Olivia had made a large collage of those volcano images, and framed them, and it hung in the front hallway, a strange greeting when you entered the house, so cozy in all its details, the pictures of that lava-spewing crater like a fierce warning the rest of the house belied.

Of course Gulaga itself was a volcano once, but you don't think of that as you make the walk to the top, through the eucalyptus forest that gives way to rainforest to cloud forest to the scrub at the pinnacle: a mountain so alive and fertile, it is hard to imagine that it once breathed fire and death.

I have been reading the Zen sutras in Narooma. *Things are not as they seem, nor are they otherwise,* the Buddha said. Maybe Olivia was a Zen master in disguise, leaving me koans to last lifetimes, each breath itself a mystery bridge from one incarnation to the next.

The nurse who discovered her dead said her face was peaceful and happy, *as if she had heard a funny story and then slipped off.*

Slipped off to where? I asked Eve, who repeated the nurse's consoling words to me as I bawled. *Slipped off to where?*

What could she say? Not Heaven. Not sleep. Not oblivion, at least to me, just a child for whom such a harsh vision would be punishing. *We don't know where she's gone,* is what she said, and now I know she was speaking of herself and of me, as much as she was of Olivia. All three of us *slipped off,* leaving behind those who have repeated for years the words that have become a chant, a wail, a prayer and a plea: *We don't know where she's gone. We don't know where she's gone. We don't know where she's gone.*

She had designated us *next of kin* in her will, and none of her actual family – her cousin Thomas, or George's siblings – challenged that. If townspeople ever had doubts we were related or scoffed at our sense of ourselves as a family, these contentions seemed to be put to rest at the funeral. She wanted it *a non-religious service* at the funeral home in Narooma, and asked that she be cremated *because I'm not interested in taking up space where someone could grow vegetables instead.* I doubt the solicitor who read the will to us in his office above the barbershop had ever come upon one as irrepressibly personal as Olivia's.

She had bought one of those template forms in the newsagent's and filled it out herself, at home. I had seen her doing it one day, years before she died, at the dining room table where I am writing now. When I'd asked her what *she* was writing, she'd said, *It's a will, Nella. They call it that because it is the last time you get to say I will, and I absolutely will not.* She winked at me, but from the straightness of her posture as she sat at her task, I realized there was something serious in these final declarations.

Do you think I should write a will, too? I asked.

Well, she said. *You could. Nothing says you couldn't. But most people wait awhile. Until you know you've stopped growing, let's say. Or your wisdom teeth have cut through. I'd put it on hold for awhile if it were me.* And so I did. But that phrase, *the last time,* landed in my heart and vibrated there, making a deep mark. For each of us, there would be *a last time.* It was as if she had given me information never before spoken, or maybe it had been, and I wasn't alert.

A kind of somber light moved into view and seemed to color everything from then on. As if everything I was noticing was being seen through the scrim of its ending, which made all of the world more precious and more fragile and made it more urgent that I set down what I witnessed. I think the writer in me was born at that moment, and sits here now, giving word to all that has ended, known and unknown, left in will and letter, in memory and dream, grasped in waking light and gleaned in the dark of sleep.

Before our neighbors arrived for the funeral, and Thomas, the cousin from Tasmania, and George's sister from Perth, Eve and I were ushered into a small room behind the chapel. Floral-patterned wallpaper, plush carpet on the floor, a vase of white lilies on a corner table: a space made to feel like a tiny guest room where the visitor was welcomed and cared for as she slept through the night or snoozed in the daytime. Except that this guest would sleep forever and there would be no breakfast in the kitchen once she arose, or scones fresh from the oven waiting on the table for afternoon tea.

Olivia lay in a plain coffin, and, confusingly, she looked just like herself, taking a nap on a warm summer day. Maybe it was make-up, or the way the light shone through the window on to her still face, but she just didn't look dead, in the way I had seen in photos of dead people in magazines. It seemed bizarre, and not a little cruel, that we had come to say good-bye forever to someone who looked as reliably alive as she always had. For some moments, I feared she had been designated *deceased* by accident, and that I needed to sound an alarm and save her from being murdered in the crematorium.

That was before I touched her hand – as soon as I felt that cold and pulseless flesh, I knew that it was true: she had changed from one kind of person to another, from the kind called *alive* to one announced as *dead.* I say *touched her hand*, but actually the effect was the opposite. It was as if that hand had moved to meet mine, had summoned my touch as if by a magnet embedded in the glass-like skin, had needed to give me proof of what I was questioning.

Later in my life, I would hear about the spirit leaving the person the moment death arrives, how you look down onto the bed, and the body you see is not the living human being you knew, but rather a vase from which the flowers disappear, or a teapot emptied of its liquid, or a planter from which someone has made off with the fern that had thrived in it for years. But that was not what Olivia was like, dead. If something had fled her body, ascended out of the top of her head, flowed out through her feet – some essence without which she would appear to be a mannequin or replica, lying there in the pine box – it was not apparent to me. Only the hand indicated what the rest of her seemed to deny, but the hand was enough.

She looks like herself, Eve said.

She spoke with the voice of one who has known the dead person a lifetime, rather than ten years, but of course Eve's life as Eve had only begun ten years ago, and so, like me, it was a lifetime's knowing she was summoning. She bent over Olivia, kissed her on the forehead, then took my hand and we walked out into the chapel, where neighbors and family more distant than us had gathered.

That was the moment I understood it was just Eve and me now, that we were a household of two rather than three, and that Olivia was never going to make oatmeal cookies again, or plant a new wattle in the corner of the yard where a windstorm had brought down the old one, or sing the entire score from *South Pacific* while she cleaned the house.

I could feel the details of her presence fading from the world. It seems we make a person real by what we can predict of their actions, memory seeding the future, each of us keeping one another living by what we trust the other will say or do. Aboriginals sing the land alive, and perhaps that ritual – the dreaming – is more universal than we know. Perhaps we are all dreaming each other into being, and dreaming each other out.

All my life, without my knowing it, my parents and sister on the other side of the world were imagining me as a baby and child and young woman and ageing adult, and their visions of the lost Naomi have been part of the air that I, Nella, have breathed. If they had given me up for dead, and closed their dreaming of me down, I might have joined Olivia long ago in the grave.

A celebrant Olivia knew from her volunteer work at the Animal Refuge one day a week conducted a ten-minute service, during which she read a letter which Olivia had written, thanking us all *for being in my life and letting me love you.* George's sister from New Zealand, Etta, sang Olivia's favorite show tune, *You'll Never Walk Alone,* and nobody mentioned God, nobody bowed a head. There were tears, and boxes of tissues throughout the chapel in the way you would put out plates of spring rolls and curry puffs at a party.

Afterwards, everyone gave us their sympathies, hugging first my mother and then me. If townspeople ever had doubts we were related, or scoffed at our sense of ourselves as a family, these contentions seemed to be put to rest at the funeral. Nick, the Montague naturalist and guide, brought his nephew, Alex. Alex didn't hug me – a boy of twelve, allergic then to sentiment, especially in public – but he looked into my eyes in a way that met me so fully, I had to lower my gaze. I had the sense then that we were very close without ever having had a proper conversation, or my even knowing his last name. This felt good and also strange, as it does to this day.

And then we all went back to the house for the post-funeral lunch.

In her will, Olivia left the house to Eve, and instructions for the ceremony, and the lunch afterwards at home, and details about where she wanted her ashes buried – right in the back yard, at the base of the gum tree which looked out to Gulaga, though the washing blocked the view a bit when the clothes were drying on the Hills Hoist. George, it turned out, was right there too, minus the small portions of ashes she'd sent to his siblings, we learned at her funeral from the Perth sister, in plastic sandwich bags, each one wrapped in one of his cotton plaid handkerchiefs she'd tied up with twine, encased in bubble-wrap and posted inside a padded mailing envelope.

12

How strange it was to return to the house without Olivia living in it. In some ways, we were prepared for her death – the illness, the hospital, the fatal diagnosis. A woman in her seventies – not entirely unnatural. But at 2 Tamarind Road, a hole opened up, and for the next years, Eve and I circled it as if it were a crater in the lounge room, roped off with tape that warned *DANGER* in day-glo orange. One might imagine that Olivia's death would have brought me closer to the only mother I have known, but in fact we each withdrew from the other.

What did we fear? Eve no doubt missed the buffer Olivia provided between us, so that she could have *some space,* as she called it, when she needed to go to her room to be alone. I had always thought it was because her work left her drained, tending to so much suffering and dying, or to recover from the sadness she carried about my dead father and her lost American life, but now I realize how exhausted she must have been by the effort required to never slip up.

And I was afraid of the guilt I felt at missing Olivia as much as I did, as if it were a rebuke to Eve: *You are not as much fun, you don't listen as well, I like her cooking better than yours.* The burden of my betrayal sat heavily on my heart. Unable to forgive Eve for being herself, I was unable to forgive myself for missing Olivia as much as I did. This confusion of feelings sometimes made me ill. For the first months of my mourning, I was plagued with stomach bugs, sinus infections, sore throats and rashes. I missed a lot of school and when I didn't, I often came home at 3:30 and took a two-hour nap. Other children were outside playing, or having their piano lessons, and I was under the covers sound asleep. My appetite waned. I had no name for my suffering other than *sick again*, and I began to believe in my own frailty.

Eve bought me tonics, herbs, vitamins. She fixed me egg-nog and milkshakes to *build you up*. She had the doctor investigate everything – parasites, ulcers, Crohn's Disease. Everything other than *grief*. That was not a word we spoke, nor a condition we understood ourselves to be experiencing and with which we might need help. And how could it have been otherwise? A life established in silence, a past never to be invoked, secrets we each protected and questions that could not be asked; rather than challenging that unspoken pact, Olivia's death strengthened it. When, in time, my symptoms abated and Eve's anxiety lessened, it may have seemed that we had found a way of being together that seemed comfortable enough, but we were, in fact, dedicated to denial.

Which, of course, had always been the case, though I would not know it for another thirty-four years.

For months, we didn't go into Olivia's bedroom. Then one Saturday morning, Eve said, *It's time,* and opened the door. She was carrying a box of heavy-duty trash can liners. I followed her into the room. Absence transforms a space without changing a thing. It was the air itself that was altered, not like the harsh smokiness after a fire, but more like a faint fume rising from all of the untouched belongings, as if they too had died and were giving off a vapor that accompanied the first stages of their decomposition.

From the wardrobe, Eve began taking Olivia's dresses and blouses and gypsy skirts off their hangers and piling them on the bed. Her blue jeans with elastic waists. Her yellow terry-cloth bathrobe. The grass-stained tennis shoes, brown laced oxfords, her sandals and the red galoshes. Her cable-stitched cardigan. Her trackpants and hooded jacket. From the chest of drawers, Eve filled one whole bag with underwear, socks, flannel nightgowns and lightweight cotton ones.

My memory catalogued each piece, as if I would be asked to report one day on what had been removed. Eve didn't keep anything for herself, and didn't ask me what I might like, and I didn't know I could have claimed some garments as keepsakes. Like a thief, it seemed, while Eve was stuffing Olivia's entire wardrobe into garbage bags, I took a few pieces of Olivia's costume jewelery from the wooden bowl where she kept them on her dresser and put them in my pocket. She had called them *my pretty things,* these shiny thrift-shop bargains, and though she'd rarely wore any of it, she'd liked to know they were in the bowl, as if one day she might have had the occasion to wear the rhinestone earrings or the opal pendant or the silver bangle bracelets or the gold panda pin. There was more, but those were the pieces I scooped up while Eve was packing. I still have them, the pendant on a black cord, a talisman, around my neck as I write.

In two hours, Olivia's room was stripped bare, her belongings ready for the Salvo's thrift shop where she had bought most items in the first place. Eve was efficient, even clinical, not uttering a word as she worked, but as she closed the door behind us – *All right,* she said, *it's done now* – I heard her voice break and when I looked up at her, her eyes had flooded with sudden tears. I reached up to comfort her, but she stepped away from my touch.

I helped her put the bags in the Holden. She drove off to the donation bin in the church carpark a few blocks from our house, and after that went off to do the grocery shopping. I went into the emptied room. It didn't look different – the bed was still made, covered with Olivia's patchwork quilt, the sheer tie-back curtains still on the window, the window-shades half-raised; I could see our washing on the Hill's Hoist out back, behind it a stand of golden wattle she had planted in front of the fence, and beyond the wattle, Gulaga, the sacred mountain silvery-green in that morning's light.

I looked at myself in the bevelled-edge mirror over the drawers and saw the girl Olivia loved. And saw the tears shining on my cheeks and felt my heart shuddering in its bony cage. I lay down on Olivia's bed and the sobs came forth like a river breaking through a dam, the bed a raft I clung to as the flood of sorrow overtook the room.

Eve found me, spent, asleep on the patchwork quilt. She left me a tuna sandwich and a glass of milk and a brownie on a tray on the night-stand where Olivia used to put her book, detective stories she loved to read *because it's good to remember that things do add up in life,* she told me once, *when mostly it feels like they don't.*

I woke up mid-afternoon, ate the lunch Eve had prepared for me, and after that my illnesses grew less and less frequent. Olivia's room remained as it had been, with the cupboard and the drawers emptied of her possessions, but the furniture still exactly where it had been, and her needlepoint flowers on the walls, and the coat tree where she used to hang her shawls and hats. I started hanging my own there, like new growth returning to branches shorn of their leaves by a storm.

For many months after that day, whenever I felt myself feeling sad, instead of sickness moving in, I would make sure Eve was at work or otherwise not at home, and I would lie down on top of the patchwork quilt. Then images of Olivia would play before me as if I were in a movie theatre watching scenes and fragments of scenes projected on to the wall. Sometimes tears would come, sometimes trembling, sometimes a longing I could not appease. Sometimes sounds, raw and guttural, an animal's freeing herself from a trap. I cried and shook and hungered and growled until the sensations exhausted themselves. I would not have used the word *grief* for what I was feeling, or *catharsis* – I was eleven, words still lived close to flesh and bone, to the knowledge of the senses in their own literal tongue. I just knew I wasn't *coming down with something again,* as Eve would say. Something natural and necessary was happening to me, strange though it was.

Decades later, fulfilling the psychic's prophesy – *Something like convulsions might arise,* Serena had said; *fevers and pain are not uncommon; temporarily you could lose the power of speech* – I would remember my girlhood mourning on Olivia's bed, and how yet again the body had become the field for wounding and recovery.

Now, too, another round sears and solaces, injures and heals.

Hard labor, this writing. Naomi Gordon, being birthed a second time.

13

Nella Gilbert.

My teachers knew me as quiet, diligent, obedient and intelligent. *She always turns in her homework on time. She is polite in class.* The children thought me shy, and perhaps a little strange. I was the girl without a father, who spoke a hybrid Australian and American tongue, who wasn't good at sport – but I didn't feel like an outcast. I learned how to fit in, even if the place where I fitted was not with the popular or adventurous. I had a little tribe I belonged to on the playground at recess. We were the shy ones, the awkward ones, the brainy introverts more comfortable inside a book than at the chip shop, buying a greasy bag to take down to the harbor, where other children gathered like water-birds in blue-uniformed flocks, their chatter as constant as the gulls who eyed the picnic tables and waited for the scraps or, if they were lucky, a whole bag of fried potato chips dropped on the ground by a boy lunging in jest for another, or a girl knocking her bag into the sand when she looked for a mirror in her schoolbag in order to check her hair. I watched them sometimes, those social children, from a safe distance under a tree where I pretended to wait for a friend who never arrived.

I was good at living *as if*, impersonating myself, as it were, pretending to be one Nella while another hid inside. And, of course, I had the perfect teacher in *as if*, Eve schooling me every day in just this kind of make-believe, her façade so perfectly maintained, she must have fooled herself most days. If police had appeared to question her, she would have been truly shocked, I have come to believe, Ruth buried within as thoroughly as if someone else were harboring her, sheltering a felon, gifted at subterfuge and disguise.

One day a friend did arrive, in the year 5 class. I was ten. Her name was Alice Martoni, the new girl. They came from Sydney, leaving the comfort of a big-city Italian neighborhood for the quieter pace of a small town on the South Coast. When I say Alice was a *real* friend, I mean we weren't just friends at school, but afterwards too, walking home the three blocks to my house and then two more to hers, stopping at the corner store for a Cherry Ripe or a Mars Bar. Alice was taller than me, by a head, but I was older, by four months. She had red hair she wore in plaits, mine was black and short and shiny, like Eve's, one of the few ways we resembled each other. *You favor your father's side,* she used to say, wistfully. And then the stiffness in her body, the barrier she became against any questions I might have: *Why don't you have any photos? Where do his family live? Why don't they ever write or call?*

What did Alice and I talk about as we made our way together down the familiar streets of our neighborhood? We compared mothers: *My mother is a nurse and my father is dead* and *Mine stays home because my father's an electrician.* We confided secrets: *I fed my pet turtle a dead spider,* I said, and Alice said, *I put on my mother's lipstick and walked around in her high heels.* We gossiped: *Lizbeth got detention because she pushed Sylvie on the playground,* and *I saw Mrs. Brady put a stick of chewing gum in her mouth after school one day.* We lied: I told Alice *My mum has a cousin in the United States who is famous movie star* and Alice said *When we go to Italy to see where my grandparents were born, I am going to have lunch with the Pope.*

Alice lived with her family in a house a lot like ours from the outside – single-story brick veneer, tidy garden, veggies growing out back, a Hill's Hoist on which laundry dried in the sea breeze most days. Inside, though, the differences were clear. The Martonis were modern, is how I would say it. Their furniture looked like the kind you would have found new in a shop window, matching lounges in an up-to-date brown suede, a glass-topped coffee table, overhead lights with dimmer switches, a television inside a wardrobe they'd close up to hide the screen when nobody was watching it, a dining room where all the teak chairs matched the long teak table that could seat twelve when they put in both leaves unlike our round maple one with four chairs each a different style from one yard sale or another, Olivia's way of home-making when she was a young bride of limited means, and never did get around to changing anything when finances improved. The Martoni walls were painted beige rather than wall-papered in old-fashioned prints like ours, and on those painted surfaces, dozens of family photographs hung in groups and rows, so that the house seemed full to the brim with company even when only Alice was there with her two parents, two brothers, a cat who went in and out through a little door in the laundry. There were grandparents on both sides who also lived in town and came and went as if the house was theirs, too, along with aunts and uncles and cousins – no wonder they had such a big table, and had to add a folding one as well for Sunday lunch. It struck me once that the cat was like me: coming to visit the house and pretending to be one of the Martonis, but then leaving through the special door and going back to her life in the gum tree bush.

I didn't know then that Alice's father went to AA meetings in the Uniting Church basement on Wednesday nights. I didn't know that her mother once packed suitcases for herself and her children and even called the taxi to take them to Bermagui, where her sister Frances lived. But when the taxi arrived, Mrs. Martoni burst into tears and sent it away, and said to Alice and her brothers, *I must have lost my mind for a minute.* They were all still on the verandah, sitting on their luggage while their mother wept, when Mr. Martoni drove the Holden into the driveway. When he saw that his family had been on the verge of leaving, Alice would tell me years later, instead of locking himself in his shed, which is what he usually did when he felt anger about to overtake him, he fell to his knees in front of his weeping wife and begged her to forgive him and started going to AA the very next day. But she never really trusted that he was sober and searched the house for bottles when he was at work the way some women polish the silver: just one of my mother's chores.

So, it turned out, Alice had been pretending to have a happy family, just as I was pretending to be a Martoni to myself, those afternoons of my girlhood. Not because I didn't love Eve and Olivia. I did. But because I yearned for a clan, a whole tribe who looked like one another and ate the same foods and told stories about *the old country:* a history celebrated rather than erased. *As if.*

And years later, I would discover that, just like Alice Martoni, I'd had an expert tutor in living *as if:* a mother who wasn't my mother or anyone else's, a widow who had invented the husband she never had, a woman who impersonated herself from the moment she woke up until she laid her head down at night. Perhaps even her dreams were rehearsals and auditions and elaborate staged productions. Perhaps she never knew a moment of authenticity from the day she took me until the day she died.

Sometimes I trust that when she wrote me her letter, it was a genuine gesture. That it was her redemption, her retirement from pretense, the end of her lies.

That she turned herself in, so to speak, to me.

That she accepted my verdict: guilty as charged.

That she surrendered, and in so doing, was released.

Who, when, where, what and why.

For years, this is how I have taught my students to assemble a narrative. Each memory of a life, each puzzle-piece of the ancestral tale. A checklist of the essential components that keep the fly-away pieces together, that gather in the details, like your grandmother's apron held the apples she was peeling for the turnovers you will remember all your years.

I'm stuck on *why.* I've read Eve's letter a thousand times, and the pages rest in my hands like a pile of leaves. Soon they'll turn to powder in my palms, and her motive – *I was compelled* – will be lost to me like dust to a sudden wind.

This just comes: perhaps it isn't Eve's *why* that's needed here, but mine. Why do I persist in this interrogation, this genealogy, this archival enterprise? Why I am writing down the *what, when, where and how?*

If we have a child, I said to Alex, *wouldn't you want her or him to know the truth?*

That's what they robbed me from, he said. *The truth.*

Not theirs, Alex. Yours, yours.

Not yours, Eve. Mine.

Here is her letter, written on blue vellum stationery with a deckle edge, paper she would have bought at the news agent's, in a see-through plastic box. The kind of paper women of her time used for notes of thank-you, congratulations, sympathy, cheery greetings with recipes included for a new dessert, apologies for lapses: *Forgive me for forgetting your birthday* or *I have just now learned of your dear mother's death.* Or, in this case, *I need to let you know that I am your kidnapper, not your mum at all, and here are the real facts of your parentage, forty-odd years after I stole you away.*

Here is her letter, which at first I dismissed as delirium, then disparaged as some cruel joke, then interrogated syllable by syllable as if a written text might yield the flesh-and-blood intention that birthed each word. And then the months of research, the verifications, the archival collecting: birth certificate facsimiles, immigration records, social security documentation, phone book listings, obituaries and birth announcements, police reports, newspaper accounts of a terrible crime.

Here is her letter, *To Be Opened Upon My Death* written in her careful hand on the blue vellum envelope.

Here is her letter, which I know so well by now, it's as if I had written it myself:

Dear Nella,

I never thought I would write this letter. You would be so hurt. That's how I thought about it. I had your interests at heart, like a mother does. Now that I have the diagnosis, Stage 4, I see things differently. They give me a month. I can see now that I owe it to you, to tell you the truth. At the nursing home, I saw it all the time, people on their death beds confiding life-long secrets, confessing, forgiving and asking for forgiveness. Never thought it would be me, but here I am now, just the same as my patients.

When you were three days old, I took you from the new-born nursery in Mercy Hospital, Pittsburgh, in America. At the end of my shift, I lifted you up from your bassinet and put you in a sling I was wearing under my raincoat. You were sound asleep and didn't even whimper. Janey, the other nurse on duty, always signed out ten minutes before me so she could get the 6:58 bus, when the night-duty girls were just coming in. I always covered that gap, waiting for them, but this time I used it as my opportunity. Quicker than changing a diaper. We were through the employees exit before the night nurses even came on the floor. For that short time, the other babies were alone. That has weighed on me. I hope there were no emergencies. It wasn't something I even thought about, that one day I would have to tell you the truth. I was so fixed on my plan. I brought you to Australia and raised you as my own. Your real parents are Paul and Deborah Gordon. She was in Room 32B. They named you Naomi. I changed it to Nella when I took you away.

All I can say is I was compelled. That is the word that comes to me. It is not even a word I would normally use. COMPELLED. But it is the word that comes. I am sorry if this is hard to follow, I am writing the way I would talk to you, if I were brave enough.

Eve is not my real name. I was born Ruth Miller, in Pittsburgh, the child of Gilbert and Sophie. They had another child first, Chana, but they lost her as a baby, in Europe during the war. Somehow my parents survived — they would never talk about it. My parents are the same people as the ones in the photo on the piano, but their names are not William and Lucy Gilbert.

In Poland, their name was Milofsky. In March 1946, a clerk at Ellis Island changed it to Miller. Ellis Island is off New York, and it's where refugees got checked in when they came to America. If they didn't know how to spell the Jewish name they heard the person say, they gave him or her an easier one. My father used to say that he should have insisted on Milofsky. What's so hard about that name, he would say. Others kept it, why not him? But he didn't. And then it was too late to change it back. The citizenship papers, the Social Security card, the driver's license, the rental lease: Miller it was, Miller it stayed. I don't know if my mother cared. She never said. And what her name was before she married my father, she never said. Now that I think of it, they kept their past a secret from me as much as I have kept mine from you.

I don't know why they settled in Pittsburgh. Maybe the Jewish Relief Agency sent them there. Maybe a friend from their town wound up there before the war, and they remembered the neighborhood, Squirrel Hill, where this friend had settled in 1932. So after the war, they went there too. Maybe the friend sponsored them. They never said. We had no other family, there or anywhere. Just the three of us. In Squirrel Hill, many others had lost everyone, not just my parents. It was natural to start over, which meant the children never asked questions. We knew not to. We were here. Here. And we were happy. A happy family. That is what stands out.

I could go on at length about our happy times. I don't have pictures. I destroyed the albums before we left for Australia.

Not that you would want them now. Because they are not your real grandparents and I am not your real mother. To write those words, I can hardly breathe. But in case you still think of us as your family, I am giving you some background.

You and I were all over the newspapers. When they put two and two together. Once I went into a newsagent's in Sydney, right after we arrived, and there were our photos, in the Wall Street Journal which the rich people like to read here, I guess. Money is money, all over the world. You can imagine how I felt when I saw those pictures. Someone would notice and turn us in. I took you right back to the boarding house where we were living then, and we didn't go outside for three days. I pretended you were sick and the woman who owned the place brought us food and formula. I waited for police to pound on the door. But they never did. Not even the newsagent, who had those photos staring right at him all day, put two and two together. I had dyed my hair. That changes appearance a lot. After that, I stopped being afraid we would be found. I knew the plan had worked.

The Pittsburgh police would have figured out I was the one who took you once I didn't come back to work. Or maybe that night they knew and got to the airport just after our plane took off. I am sure they went over my apartment with a fine-tooth comb. Not that I had anything of much interest or value. I am a very ordinary person. But it all would have become evidence. I remember once thinking I wish I could see the file on me, because maybe it would help me understand why I did what I did. They never found us, of course. In those days I think there were more holes in the net. It was easier to disappear.

My parents ran to Pittsburgh, and after they died, I ran from there to Sydney. I never thought I would run like they did, from one country to another, but I did. I used to wonder how it was possible to pick up and go from one side of the ocean to the other. But that is what I did. I looked at a World Atlas, and saw that Australia was as far as I could go, not counting Antarctica. In the library, I checked out a special issue of National Geographic, lots of pictures of the outback and the Kimberley and the Great Barrier Reef. But a normal place, too, with hospitals and such. I could get work. And the same language, not that I ever have picked up a lot of Aussie slang. I saved for the ticket for more than a year. I won't say I was always planning, that is not how it was. But something in me made a plan. Something in the background. Who knows how I figured it all out? So many details. The airline tickets, the false passports, the locker in the airport, the hair dye, the pancake makeup for your butterfly birthmark, the sling.

While I was planning, I still got up every morning and put on my uniform and went to work in the hospital. This was my life. I never married. I had beaus, we called them then, but never a proposal. I don't know why. So much I don't understand to this day. Something about me the men didn't like enough, or trust. Something they picked up, I guess. I was a pretty girl, and polite. I was sure I would get married and be a mother. Who knows why things turn out as they do? After a while, you give up asking and just live the life you have.

I had the nursing, and my parents to look after, until they died, and friends, though once their babies started coming, there wasn't much place for a single girl like me.

So, I got used to being alone a lot. I had the tv, and my magazines, and such. Every now and then a good cry, or one of those headaches just like my mother was prone to. In bed for a day, blind with pain, and my thinking turned to mud.

And then one evening, after a migraine, finally getting up to make a scrambled egg and a cup of black tea, which is what I could keep down, things fell into place. At least it felt like that to me. Like I was being given instructions. A plan all laid out, like somebody else had drawn it up and was whispering it into my ear. Nurses obey, we are trained in that. What the doctors say to do, we do. What the procedures are, we follow them. I just did as I was told. Some things we can't understand. I don't try.

You are probably thinking, why should I believe a word she says?

That is a good question. That will be your puzzle, how to know what to make of anything in this letter. You are a smart girl. You will start to ask questions. Records are easy to find. Articles in the papers. And so forth.

You will search for the Gordons, of that I'm sure. I am sure they have been searching for you.

The police will help. Cases like mine, they are never closed. In the end, things will be put right. I have nothing more to add. I hope you can forgive me. I doubt that you will.

Your mother, Eve

14

Your mother, Eve.

She left the letter for me in the second drawer of the maple nightstand beside her bed. I had brought her home from the hospital, after a week of scans and the diagnosis and her decision to forego the chemo and the radiation. They might be able to shrink the tumors, they said, buy her a few more months. She declined. *Nurses know,* she said. *We don't go in for the treatments that much, when it's terminal. We just want the pain relief. Why add misery to misery?*

Back on Tamarind Road, I helped her into her bed and she stayed there more and more over the next five weeks. I imagine she wrote me her letter soon after arriving home, when she still had a bit more energy, and someone wasn't at her bedside every moment. Wrote the letter, sealed in its envelope and set it in the drawer the way one might hide a bomb on a timer. The letter lay there beneath a half-dozen pair of neatly folded support stockings that she'd worn every day to work at Pelican Cove. Eve would never wear the stockings again, and so the drawer remained untouched during the weeks of her dying, safe from anyone who might discover what she had hidden there.

A hospice nurse came by that first afternoon and set up the morphine drip on the pole Eve now walked with wherever she went, while she still could walk. The nurse would be there every day at 3 p.m. She taught me what I had to know: the toileting, the soft diet while Eve still was eating food, the way to massage her hands and feet. The signs to watch out for – hemorrhaging, dehydration, hallucinations – in case I needed emergency help, but I never did.

Neighbors brought soups and cakes and stayed for brief awkward visits. A few co-workers came from Pelican Cove, and one day they sang for her, the way she had joined them in the nursing home when a patient was dying there. By now Eve was in bed all the time. *You'll Never Walk Alone* and *Climb Every Mountain* were their favorites, and that's what they sang to Eve now. She lay there with her eyes closed as they sang, and you might have thought she was oblivious to the singers, or indifferent, but I did notice how one hand kept time on top of the other, just under the sheet.

I was alone with my mother, Eve, as she died. Alex would have been with me, had that been possible. Of course, it was not. And yet I did feel him, sometimes, during those days and nights, as if by my side. Once I was so sure he had entered the room that I called him by name, and Eve said, *Why would you talk to a ghost, Nella?* and then: *Oh my, I see him, too!* I lay a wet cloth on her forehead, to calm her hallucination. When actually I was the one who had taken us into the territory of mirage or superstition or genuine encounter with his spirit, I cannot say which.

Eve seemed to be turning outside-in, whatever was on the surface becoming a husk, a shell, an abandoned cocoon. I watched her vanish into herself, and on to wherever consciousness moves, and finally the body there in the bed was no longer my mother. *Your mother, Eve.* Even before she died, she died.

Not her first vanishing by far, but I had not known of any other then. For days, I grieved her as a daughter would, and when her letter exploded all I thought I knew about love and loss, my sorrow deepened, but for whom or what, I was unsure.

Because I am trying to understand the missed clues, the hidden evidence, the signs in plain sight I never saw, I can see how my narrative focuses on Eve's reserve and secrecy, the force-field of privacy she created around herself. It might seem that Olivia was the real mother in that house, and Eve a kind of visiting relative or a boarder who I liked enough, but with whom I never bonded.

Not true.

And not enough to say *I loved her,* and then return to documenting the distances between us, the ways I now see her evasions as subterfuge, her silences a kind of Fifth Amendment refusal to incriminate herself. If she had never written me her letter of confession, if I had never come to know the truth of my birth and abduction, I would have a different story to tell, a happier one, one more attuned to all the ways we were close, the trust I felt, the ways in which I valued her.

My mother is a wonderful woman, I would say, and so I will say that now. She was a wonderful woman. That evidence needs to be included too. That testimony, valid as any I might swear to in a court of law, or on my own deathbed, wanting the truth to be available in all its contradictions.

An early memory of Eve: I am in a child's plastic wading pool in our Narooma backyard on a hot summer day, and she is kneeling beside me on the grass. I'm about two, it feels like. One by one, she's offering me rubber animals to take into the water, and she's made up a song to accompany the play: *Here's a puppy, here's a cat, here's a giraffe in a great top hat. Here's a birdie, here's a bug, here is Mummy giving Nella a hug!* And then reaching into the pool to embrace me, both of us laughing, water splashing all over Eve, which makes us laugh even more.

Thinking of this now, I see she was surprisingly good at that kind of silly play. It called her out of her guarded reserve into an eternal childhood in which both of us delighted in the other. In those moments, she wasn't teaching me anything, or watching her words, or on guard for questions that might trip her up as surely as if I were to pull a mask from her face.

On Sunday mornings, curling up with her in her bed while Olivia cooked bacon and eggs, French toast with maple syrup, fresh-baked biscuits we would all savor together at the table. *A day off for both of you*, Olivia insisted, so we luxuriated in her generosity. In bed, Eve and I played games like Twenty Questions, and Scissors / Rock / Paper, Fingers and Toes. She read me books – her favorites were Dr. Seuss when I was little, Louisa May Alcott as I got older. Once I started going to the library, I'd bring her the book I had chosen myself and cuddled with Mum – because I called her Mum, remember, not Eve – while she read to me in her dulcet voice – yes, she had a beautiful voice, which her patients at the nursing home must have found soothing and kind – which I can hear now as I write.

And because she was a nurse, I always felt protected and cared for when I was sick. I was prone to chest colds and sinus attacks. Home a lot from school, or so it seemed. Though she worked, Mum would awaken herself early to make sure my medicines were arranged on my bedside table, and a bouquet of flowers from the garden outside she would pick each morning, and notes she would leave me: *To my darling Nella, get lots of rest today and enjoy these flowers, just for you to help you feel better* or *Darling Nella, Mum will be thinking of you all day and sending you buckets of love.* She would phone me at lunch-time, and sometimes when I answered she would imitate Donald Duck, which dissolved me into laughter, no matter how sick I had been feeling. On the way home, she would stop at the market to pick up some sweet treats I loved – double chocolate ice cream in tiny containers with a wooden spoon, a bottle of orange soda, a bag of pretzels. *Here's a secret,* she confided once, in fun. *When you're sick, the snacks that are bad for you turn into medicine. Only nurses know about this. Isn't that wonderful?!*

When Mum was tired after a day of work, she didn't have much energy for play, whether I was sick or well. But what she did offer was a space beside her on the sofa – she would pat the cushion next to her as invitation and request. She'd read the *Shoalhaven Times*, or the latest issue of *Women's Day* magazine, or work on the crossword puzzle from the *Sunday Herald.* But one arm was around my shoulder, or massaging my scalp, or beside her, holding my hand while we shared companionable *quiet time,* she called it.

Sometimes, on Sundays, all the years of my girlhood, from toddler to young woman, soon to leave for university, we'd go on walks together. There were the ones I already wrote about, when I began collecting the treasures that I stored in the bookcase she bought me as display shelving. Other times, in the afternoon when Olivia was taking her nap, I went with Eve to a part of the beach we both loved, and we'd walk for kilometers, watching the sun move across the water, and the tide come in. At Apex Park along the boardwalk where fresh fish were scaled and cleaned, we watched the pelicans gather in droves. We took photos of them at the Town Wharf on Bluewater Drive or around Forsters Bay – flocks of the great white birds like magnets for Mum and me. I would learn later in life that pelicans are symbols in mythology for devoted mothering, how in time of famine they peck their breasts for blood with which to feed their babies. She was a good photographer, and I still have what she called The Pelican Albums, which she arranged chronologically on a bookcase shelf in the lounge room. Red leather covers, and the photos mounted under plastic sleeves in which each page sat. Our own private ornithology, a mother-daughter effort, all those years the kidnapped child and her criminal mother loved each other in the most unremarkable, and precious, ways.

If Olivia was my playful companion and consoler, it was Mum I came to turn to for intimate advice. All the usual kinds that you might imagine. When to buy my first bra; how to shave my legs; how to prepare for *my monthlies,* as we called menstruation then. If I had a nightmare, it was Mum to whom I went for comfort. If I felt hurt by a schoolmate's rejection, I talked to Mum about my pain and she was good at receiving me as I was, without trying to talk me out of my tears or offer me endless suggestions for how to change the situation. She knew how to listen, is how I would say it now. Will say it now: *my mother was a good listener.*

Is it clear now I could write an entire volume of tribute to Eve/Ruth/Mum? I could. Is that what drives me now, here in my childhood home, in which the grenade of her letter exploded? No, what drives me now is the truth I missed, not the truth I knew. But the truth I knew needs to be recorded, because only then does the truth I missed shock with its now-visible detail, and how it lived hidden from me, at once in plain sight and dark obscurity, all the years I knew myself as Nella Gilbert and my mother as Eve, the widow from Pittsburgh, Pennsylvania, in the United States, who came with me to Australia when I was an infant and made a home for us with Olivia Stroud in Narooma, where I am writing this report, this indictment, this psalm, this lament.

Unlike the aftermath of Olivia's death, how it took us months to go through her things and pack up all those bags of clothing for the Salvation Army, I decided to face the task straight-on after Eve died. Partly because I was no longer living in Narooma, but also because I had been more prepared – I was a grown woman now, I understood now how mortality claims us. I could *get on with it*, as Australians like to say. I could *carry on.*

Until I opened the nightstand drawer and found the letter with my name on the envelope.

Until the words that Eve wrote in her careful script on her blue vellum stationery with the deckled edge went off in my hands, yet somehow I and the pages remained undestroyed. I would read the letter again and again, and each time the percussive shockwaves through the body, that shattering of the mind.

And do you know what remained, once all the other words turned to dust and I could no longer understand them as meaningful code? It was this: *They had another child first, Chana, but they lost her as a baby, in Europe during the war.*

I circle round and round her name, *Chana*, as if it were a stupa, or a sacred burial site. I stand before her name as if it were the Wailing Wall. Everything else in Eve's letter falls away, and only this absent Chana persists. She is my double, my doppelgänger, my soul's twin.

Was she real? A child born and vanished? Or did Eve concoct her to plant a motive for which I might have compassion? A woman who plans a kidnapping and a flight from one side of the world to another, then decades of falsity, every little lie in place like a carefully-built clock; wouldn't she be capable, too, of a death-bed confession that's pure fiction?

Perhaps not.

I sense not.

I sense what she's written is a partial understanding of why she kidnapped me. I think that is why she spent so much of her letter writing about her parents and what they had suffered before she was born. She sees the likeness of her mother's loss and Deborah Gordon's – surely she sees that much – but she doesn't see that one recapitulates the other with unconscious intention. Repetition compulsion, as Freud would have named it, stealing me as a way Eve re-enacted her mother's loss.

I was compelled.

There, right in that word she chose, diagnosis and denouement.

Deborah Gordon ravaged as Eve's mother would have been by Chana's loss, and Chana's loss, Ruth reasoned in her unreason, made right by Eve's abduction of me. As if I were Chana in another form, and Eve her mother whose first-born has been restored to her.

(Oh, I know as a writer I should leave some of the mystery for a reader to solve, but this is not that kind of story. I am not writing fiction. *Save conclusions for a court of law,* an editor might suggest. *Let the evidence speak for itself.* But there is no court, and the evidence is mostly mute. Let me be the anti-Sphinx. I need to be my own court of law, where every speculation is spoken, evidence presented, conclusions – airtight or circumstantial – clear and necessary. A surfeit of exhibits).

Repetition, restitution, reparation.

A deluded logic driving Eve like a dream.

Compelled. This happens, we know. The mind confuses itself. I have read memoirs. I have heard such stories from my students.

In Beirut, Jamila's father would sit for hours, outside, in sun and rain, waiting for her mother, who had died when a bomb buried her under the rubble of the family home. *I need to be where she'll see me,* he said when the children begged him to come into the tent they lived in now, in a refugee camp. *I need to be visible.*

Bao, from a village in Vietnam, told the class that his grandmother used to hide his shoes on the mornings when he needed them to walk to school. *Not for a joke,* Bao told us, but because his sister had been killed by land-mine on the same walk three years before, and the grandmother reasoned that Bao would live another day if he had to stay home because he couldn't find his shoes, though he always did. *Where can you hide something in a two-room house?* he said. He smiled, and then he cried. His sister's name was Doan Vien, which meant *happy reunion.*

To avenge the theft, generations back, of seven cows on the outskirts of Khartoum, Minoo's brothers were obliged to poison the pond where the thief's descendants brought their own herd to graze. One day a child from that family fell into the pond and died from the arsenic-laced water. It was decided that Allah had extracted justice for the theft via the child's death, and the feud ended with a solemn feast which both families prepared together.

In such ways, I have learned, we are driven to live out a family curse, or to undo one. Crimes reveal themselves as distorted acts of redemption once one understands the myth of generations, a story performed for millennia until the ending changes and the family is freed. It is not unusual, of course, for such freedom to come at grave cost to another, laying down yet another curse crying out for release.

Maybe Eve was crafty enough to know I'd soften in the face of such a version, not hate her so much, not banish her from my heart.

Or maybe she was in the story's grip, the way a feverish nightmare takes hold of you for hours after you've awakened.

Or maybe she just wrote down what was true, as far as she was able to understand what that might be.

I've gone through her narrative a thousand times and it neither adds up nor doesn't.

So much of our lives impenetrable, impervious to reason, outside the bounds of verification.

I'll wager Chana did live, and die, or disappear.

A fall from a wagon in which they were fleeing. A fever from which her parents couldn't save her. A suffocation, accidental, as her mother tried to stifle her cries so they wouldn't be discovered in a hiding place. Or perhaps someone stole her, just as Eve stole me. One minute she was there in her cot, the next minute vanished. Perhaps she was handed by her parents to a rescuer who spirited her to a Polish convent who then passed her on to a Christian family's home where she was hidden during the war and raised as a good Catholic girl, her true identity lost forever in the chaos of the war. When her parents returned to the convent to reclaim her, the nuns couldn't tell her where the child had gone. They didn't keep records, or the records were destroyed. Chana might be living today in Krakow or Warsaw, an old woman with grandchildren for whom she bakes strudel after they return from Sunday morning mass.

I have searched the records, as Eve knew I would. I did find a Gilbert Miller and Sophie Miller who arrived at Ellis Island from Poland at the time Eve said they did. I did find people called Milofsky in the town of Srzyzow, though none named Gilbert or Sophie, which, as their surnames, would have likely been Anglicized versions of something else. Research tells me Gilberts had often been Sheragai in Hebrew, and Sophies derived from Tzofia, though that is more common among Sephardi, while Eve's parents were Ashkenazi. How can I authenticate what has vanished into air? All that's left is inference, deduction, imagination. Nothing recorded anywhere about a dead child. No birth certificate for a Jewish infant born into a genocide, when documentation was as good as a death sentence.

If, in America, Immigration asked if they had children, they would say no. A dead baby belonged to the dead life they fled. And maybe they would be afraid to say anything about Chana. They could have feared they would be blamed for the infant's death. Or for having abandoned her to a convent. Arrested, or sent back. They would have been frightened of everything then, especially officials in uniforms stamping their papers, letting them in or banishing them. Why would they cast any suspicion on themselves?

Perhaps they simply could not bear to say her name.

Yes, I know this is speculation, but that is how story works. From one fragment, the rest unfolds, like the gossamer of a spider's elaborate web. An overheard snippet of conversation, and the narrative emerges, as if a new planet has appeared in the universe. An amnesiac hears a word from her mother tongue, and the lost life returns, in full.

My lost life. My lost *Jewish* life. Learning of my lineage, I could only think of Alex, telling me again and again the shock he felt discovering the truth of his own birth: that his birth mother hadn't given him up willingly at all, that she had been forced to relinquish him and grieved for him all of her life.

Out of the blue. A phone call from a sister. He was twenty-five.

You're my lost brother, Lorena said. *You were stolen at birth right out of our mother's arms. She'd planned to raise you herself, but they wouldn't allow it. Sixteen years old, a Greek girl from Liverpool, right here in western Sydney.*

Out of the blue.

I didn't know anyone Jewish in Narooma. Not a soul. In Sydney, at university and then moving there to teach, I've had Jewish friends, and enjoyed the delis of the Eastern Suburbs. Once I went to Kol Nidre services at a beautiful synagogue in Woollahra with my colleague, Miriam. The night has been returning to me, again and again, since reading Eve's letter.

The idea of Yom Kippur, an entire evening and day devoted to atonement, moved me. That you would confess in a communal space all the ways you had harmed others and failed your faith. That you would seek out those you had injured and ask for forgiveness. The possibility of repair. The moral necessity of it. Without a priest or a rabbi interceding for you, absolving you, requiring penance of you. That you could do this yourself. That alone seemed a good basis for a religion, and I remember saying to my friend, after the evening service, *I could be Jewish, I think.*

Miriam invited me on the spur of the moment, after mentioning she wouldn't be at work the next day because of the Jewish holiday, and was leaving work at 4.00 for a dinner with her parents before the fast-day began, and then the service at the temple. I asked her about this holiday, out of politeness rather than interest, I knew. I did not experience myself as a religious person. But the way she described Yom Kippur reached beyond my courtesy. She must have seen that I was stirred. *Would you like to come as my guest?* she said. She knew I was suffering over the separation from Alex. *It's a very moving experience, Nella, the music goes straight to the heart.*

Straight to the heart. Mine was bruised and lonely. Alex gone then for almost a year. *Yes, I would love to, Miriam.* Something in my heart raised up, just a little, as if from a sickbed, a movement of well-being when there had been only a dull ongoing ache.

I could leave at 4.00 too, it turned out, my classes finished then for the day.

We walked together from our school in the city to the bus-stop, and the twenty-minute ride to Miriam's parents' apartment, not far from the synagogue in Woollahra. A gracious neighborhood on the edge of Centennial Park, solid brick apartment buildings, balconies blooming with potted oleander and bougainvillia and frangipani, streets lined with Moreton Bay figs and towering palms and eucaplypts in which fruit bats gathered at night, their high-pitched calls like an ancient song from another world.

Miriam's parents, Ida and Seymour, had survived Auschwitz, Miriam had told me months before. They'd met at a Displaced Persons Camp in Italy, where they recovered, if that is an applicable word, from years of torment and disease and despair. Their parents and siblings were all dead. Somehow they rescued each other from that impossible loss, and in Australia, they began a second life together, for they had died with their families in Auschwitz, as surely as if their corpses had gone up in smoke with the millions of others. When Buddhists talk of rebirth, they don't mean the kind which genocide survivors experience, one life vanished and another born within the course of single existence. But rebirth it is. Either all memory of the former life vanishes in some amnesiac fog or resurrects itself in terrible dreams each night that no sleeping pill can prevent, no cups of warm milk can ever soothe.

At dinner, I could not take my eyes off the numbers on Miriam's mother's arm. Somehow I had gone my whole life until that moment never actually seeing the tattooed brand millions were forced to endure. Ida saw that I was riveted on her number, and when she went back to the kitchen for another dish to add to the beautifully-set table, she returned with her sleeves unrolled now to her wrists and the tattoo hidden from view. I had the sense she was protecting me more than herself. But how can I know what it is like to live with such a mark, to be seen as victim, to have the rest of one's being eclipsed by the magnitude of horror to which that mark points, to turn in an instant from a complex human being into 178405? Too late, I lowered my eyes.

When the cantor sang Kol Nidre at the service that night, his tenor notes climbing to the top of the domed sanctuary, centuries of grief rode his voice, as if it were a train running backwards, away from danger and death, all the way back through history to the moment the God of the Old Testament casts out Adam and Eve from Eden.

When Alex stood in front of the house in Liverpool where his birth mother had grown up.

I joined my grief for him to the worshippers in Miriam's congregation, not knowing then I was also mourning my own birth family's losses. Which would have included me, the child taken from her parents decades before, leaving her parents and sister to wail aloud and in silence from that day until this.

That was years before I received Eve's letter, of course, years before she wrote: *Your real parents are Paul and Deborah Gordon. She was in Room 32B. They named you Naomi. I changed it to Nella when I took you away.*

As I have written: *I am the crime and the narrator-sleuth.*

As I write, it becomes clear: *I am the injury and the repair.*

In Hebrew, *tikkun.*

The language of my ancestors.

They call, they call, they call.

When I first read Eve's letter, it was as if Gulaga had erupted as it did forty million years ago, and this time it took my girlhood into its obliterating fire. As the heat subsided, I searched for relics I could retrieve. All of Olivia's remaining belongings, of course, and the house which had sheltered me and my abductor. The garden. Amazing how much remains intact, when for a time you believe all has been destroyed.

There was the photo on the piano of Gilbert and Sophie Milofsky, whom I had known as William and Lucy Gilbert, as close to a blood family other than Eve to which I'd believed I belonged. I'd come to love their faces, peering down on me in grandparental affection from the Kawai upright on which I never got much beyond *Clare de la Lune.* I'd felt especially close to Lucy – male relations were remote to me, and William never gained much dimension in my mind. I was glad to have him there, on the piano, some link to the silenced past of my family, but he didn't yield stories to my imagination. Who can say why one image remains flat and static, while another stimulates invention? Perhaps because I grew up in a house of women, it was Grandma's Lucy's image that galvanized my fantasies. Stories arose of her visits to Narooma – were they memories, I sometimes wondered, a kind of parallel household life I could enter at will? How Olivia took her in like a long-lost sister (perhaps they *were* long-lost sisters?) and planned wonderful excursions for the three of us – a bus ride to Tilba, where we'd wander among the craft shops, looking at the hand-made candles and the macramé hangings and the mirrors framed in stained-glass. Just like tourists, the three of us, while my mother Eve is working, everything as exotic to Olivia and me as it was to Lucy, I imagined, who loved to watch the wood-turners making their beautiful salad bowls and cutting boards, and the lace-workers their doilies, and the silversmiths their polished bracelets she would buy for each of us – perfect bangles that joined Eve and me and Olivia and Lucy together in a precious maternal bond. In the photo, she is barely smiling, and though you might see her image as sad, I saw a woman whose joy was just beginning to express itself when the impatient photographer snapped the camera prematurely.

By the time I was twelve, I'd made up an entire history with my dead grandparents, had they lived to know me: letters we might have exchanged, phone calls from one hemisphere to the other that would sound like underwater communication, visits I would make by ocean liner and overnight train to their home in Pittsburgh, where they would entertain me as they had my mother when she'd been young.

I didn't know what that would have been like then, but now I do.

I have researched.

I have dreamed.

Dream is an exquisite detective: you would be surprised by its accuracy. It is dreaming that allows me to construct the missing half of Eve's letter. Circumstantial evidence, you might say. Fantasy.

Or: the not-knowing that is a knowing.

She might have continued in this way:

Here we are, Nella, on a warm Sunday afternoon having a picnic in Schenley Park. Acres of grass and trails through the wooded parts. They don't walk on the trails. I want to, but my parents like to stay out in the open, they say. They have a fear of the trails, where you could disappear into the forest. I can see people coming out happy and safe. But my parents won't set foot in the woods. I was a good girl, I didn't object.

We set our blanket down on the top of Flagstaff Hill and watch the people throwing balls to their dogs. I will always remember my mother's deviled eggs. I will remember the radishes her father ate whole, like they were candy. We had pickles and tomatoes. We had salami and pumpernickel bread. A jar of dark mustard. Bottles of seltzer water. We spread everything out on the plaid woolen blanket. Other families are there, too, and the fathers have set up the volleyball net. The children have their own games: Red Rover, Statues, All Fall Down. Everyone stays until dark.

I permit myself this fiction. I have a need here for conjecture. How is that different from what the physicists do, building a universe out of inference?

If Sunday was rainy or cold, Eve might have written, *instead of a picnic, we would take the streetcar to the Phipps Conservatory. Under the glass dome, it was always summer. I liked the orchids especially. My mother said that the hundreds of flowers were like a wedding that never ends. She was a cheerful sort of person.*

Except for when Sophie is having one of her times. Maybe twice a year. She stays in her bed for days. She hardly eats. It looks like she has a flu, but she doesn't. One day, I bring her a glass of orange juice and two Lorna Doone biscuits on a plate. I remember it clear as day. I know I am ten because my birthday had just passed. I think she is talking in her sleep, but she is awake with her eyes closed. She hears me come in. She sits up with her eyes still shut. I remember she is rocking. She has her arms folded in front of her, like a cradle. Faygelah, she keeps saying, faygelah. Yiddish for baby. Then my mother looks straight at me and says: You had a sister, she died years before you were born, in Poland, two months old. It is morning, but the room is dark. She keeps the shades down all day. Some sunshine comes in around the sides, but otherwise you would think it was night. The lamp on her side of the bed is on. The way she is propped up on her pillows, the light is shining right on her heart. I will always remember that: shining right on her heart.

You had a sister, your grandmother Sophie says. She died before you were born. Two months old. We were living with my parents, of blessed memory. At the age of fifteen your father learned to be a baker from my father, and that is how the match was made. I knew him like a member of the family. Our village was Srzyzow. The Nazis came in 1939. Before that, we had a beautiful life. We had the basic needs. The wooden houses and the shops. The school, the synagogue. We had the river and forest.

Our Rabbi, she goes on, may his soul be at rest, was famous for his knowledge of the Talmud and his kindness. When he had to give a list of the males in the town who were fit for hard labor, do you know what he did? He wrote one name down, his own, and they shot him on the spot. That day, your father said we had to take the baby and run. He said he'd had a dream the night before, and none of the Jews from our town were alive — he saw every single person dead like the Rabbi. I thought I myself was dreaming, hearing him speak such a terrible thing. But when I looked into his eyes, I knew he had been instructed. That night, without saying a word to my parents, or to his family, because we knew they would oppose us, we packed a satchel with some essentials, and we gave our baby Chana some whiskey on the tongue, a dozen drops, and she fell into a sleep deeper than ever before.

We wrapped her in towels and then completely in brown paper from the bakery, with some air-holes for breathing, so it would seem she was a loaf of bread I was carrying under my arm. I asked your father, Where are we going? and he said, Far. I thought he had a place in mind, but later I would learn no, he had no place in mind, we were like animals running for our lives. People have places they go to and from. Animals, no. They are hunted and they flee.

What about my parents? I said, and he said, Your father has a bad hip and your mother the chest pain so she has to rest often. I said, We can go slow, and he said, No we can't, slow is not possible, we may as well stay here and die. And I thought I would rather stay here and die than leave my parents behind.

But Chana. Chana.

Eve would have written this in a kind of trance, of course, had she written it. How else could you release on to paper the story you have carried like an unborn child in your body for a lifetime?

I think your grandmother might be done with the story. She closes her eyes again, leans back on the pillow as if she is sick. But she manages a little more.

She says, The first night we slept in the woods. We kept giving her the whisky. I fed her from my breast when she was enough awake for the milk. We were in a cave we knew from childhood. You couldn't stand up inside it. We covered over the opening with branches and moss. Who knows how, but we slept. Before it got light again, Gilbert woke me up. He said we had to go through the woods to the dairy farmer Murawski who would hide us in the milking barn.

And then Sophie couldn't go on. Her tears came and she bowed her face down into her hands. Did they get to the Murawski farm? How long did they stay? How did they survive the war? Were they in the camps? I never heard another word about any of that, not that day or ever again. When I asked, What about Chana? my mother would start to weep. Once she did with her hands what you do to mean finished. One hand sweeps over the other like they were the blades of a scissors, making a permanent cut. I don't know if that meant died or murdered or given up forever. You had a sister, that I knew. Finished: I knew that, too. Finished.

One day, Eve might have confided in her tidy script, *I went through every drawer, clothes and linens, and the grocery cabinets, everywhere things were stored. I was looking for a record, a piece of paper, a photograph. Nothing. Okay, I decided, if it is finished for her, then it is for me, too. I was twelve, maybe, or thirteen.*

Maybe I was the first and only person she ever spoke to about Chana. Other than my father. Telling me was like having a funeral at last. That was the end of her collapses in her bed. Finished.

And I never thought of Chana again, Nella, until now, if you can believe it, writing this letter. I am 73, Stage 4. It's no surprise that what got buried comes up now, into the light of day.

It was a terrible thing that I did, Nella. A terrible thing.

There: something concrete in which her remorse might take root. Insert that section into the letter she left me, and an account I can believe in offers itself into my hands.

In the words she left me, have I found the words she held back?

And if Eve concocted Chana entirely, it is possible she did so to create for herself a narrative she herself might believe in. A fiction that pointed to a truth, rather than a lie with which to manipulate me. Something in her own history, unknown or suspected and so grievous it could only be addressed with a re-enactment trance in Mercy Hospital, just days after I was born.

This is how ritual works. One moment standing for another, a drama we invent that calls up one long forgotten and wanting to be known again, by the body if not by the mind. Crime itself is a ritual, distorted and confused, but ritual nonetheless.

You will say: *the whole thing sounds concocted, Eve's letter and your fantasy addition to it. Have you lost your mind?*

Follow my reasoning.

Even if Eve invented Chana, doing so offered her a bridge to Deborah Gordon's suffering, and Paul's, and Leah's, and to my own. Suffering that Eve had caused, and in the end, hoped to redeem.

With a story.

Because that is all she had to give. Call it a lie if you like. Or consider it a dream, a fable, a myth.

Chana lost, Naomi stolen. Two Jewish babies, vanished at birth, linked together like kin. The Millers and the Gordons united – in fact or in fiction – in an uncanny shared anguish.

Is it madness for me to participate in that leap of repair?

I am a child of both histories, learning to say my true name.

15

Teaching English to migrants was good work, and without a lot of classroom preparation and papers to mark, I reasoned, so I would have time for writing short stories.

Alex encouraged me. He said, *Stories are everything.*

I read once that the American poet, Muriel Rukeyser, wrote, *The universe is made of stories, not atoms.* I copied out that quote and hung it on the wall above my Balmain desk. When I came here to Narooma to write these pages, I unpinned the yellowed page on which I'd inscribed her words and brought it with me, in a wooden picture frame I bought for three dollars in the bargain store. It sits on the writing desk like some ancient text saved from ruin in another age. If Eve's letters exploded the world as I knew it, these stories I have salvaged might repair the damage.

Not enough to help you, Alex, though you had such faith in my tales. *Read to me, Nella,* you would say. You would open the camphorwood Chinese chest in which I kept my manuscripts. *Read to me.*

I dedicated both my collections to you.

MONTAGUE ISLAND STORIES: *For Alex, with gratitude.*

TWICE-BLESSED: *For Alex, who was a blessing, twice.*

Naomi comes alive in me, and the longing for Deborah Gordon grows.

Nella Gilbert Pine, it turns out, is a pseudonym I didn't know I was adopting. Under what name would I publish these pages, if that were my intention, which it is not?

In Sydney, I chose to live in Balmain, where I am still, not far from the boarding house where Eve took me when we arrived in Australia. How do I know she went to Balmain? How do I know about the boarding house? She didn't write about that in her letter to me. No. I heard about Balmain from conversations she had with Olivia, in the lounge room with their knitting, trading anecdotes. Why do I believe anything Eve ever said, given how much of a past I now realize she had to invent? Some things I have been able to authenticate and some things I trust because my body senses the truth of them. I have stood on the site of that first Australian home and felt the earth tremble *Yes* up through my legs and belly to the throbbing heart: *Yes, she brought you here.* Sometimes the body recognizes a lie, the details like flour passing through a sieve: a worm remains behind in the mesh, and the whole thing needs to be thrown out. Not so with the Balmain address.

Alex would have asked me all those questions, were I able to tell him about Eve's confession. I hear his voice as I write, questioning me at every turn. The year we met again, he and I hadn't seen each other since childhood, the trip to Montague Island with his Greek uncle, and then again at Olivia's funeral. He had disappeared from Narooma as mysteriously as he had arrived, and now fifteen years later, he arrived again. I didn't know anything yet about his troubled boyhood.

But always, about Alex, something like an apparition, not beside him, but there inside the man himself, as if he were part-man and part-ghost. So that when he looked at me, that doubleness looked. I found the mystery of that quality attractive. It took me time to understand how pain can sunder a man clear through, divide him from himself, how love could make the suffering worse, expose it beyond endurance, before it had any chance to heal the wound.

16

Alex said his real name was meant to be Hector. Hector, the greatest Trojan hero.

Hector Zavros, son of Daphne Zavros and her secret red-haired Irish boyfriend, Patrick O'Farrell, who worked with her after school at a milk-bar on Liverpool Street. Once, after their shift was finished, they got into his second-hand Holden and drove out to the park where Patrick knew of a hidden place behind a stand of eucalypts and dense grevillea shrubs, where he met up with mates on a weekend night to drink beer and talk about girls and sex. This was a Wednesday night, September 1967. It wasn't the first time for Patrick, but it was for Daphne. When she realized she was pregnant, Patrick quit his job at the milk-bar and told her he would ruin her reputation if she ever divulged his name as the father. *I'm a kid,* he told her. *I can't go having a kid myself.*

Alex learned about Daphne from a daughter she had: Lorena, his sister who found him twenty-five years after Daphne had been forced to sign the adoption papers without even having a chance to hold her newborn son. *She didn't tell any of us about you until she got so sick, right before she died.* A heart-valve replacement that went wrong, the heart they hoped to fix failing before she even got home from the hospital. *I think it was heartbreak that did it,* Lorena said. *No surgery can fix that, not after all those years of private grief.*

Daphne hadn't planned to give up her child. Not even when her parents sent her away to the Home down the coast, five hours from Sydney, and never coming to visit her, much like the other girls, twenty of them, children really, alone with the nuns who treated them more as delinquents remanded to their care than teenagers desperate for reassurance and mothering. Before she went to the Home, Daphne had collected baby clothes in a cardboard box she covered herself with flowered wrapping paper: three baby fleece rompers with feet, in yellow, green and white; little animal-printed T-shirts she found at a second-hand shop; a pair of crocheted booties and a matching cap, no doubt made once by a doting grandmother, say, who couldn't wait to cuddle her grandchild once the baby arrived. She kept that box with her for the rest of her life, hidden away, and only told Lorena about it when she revealed how Hector – that is how she always thought of him – was taken from her in the hospital delivery room before she even had a chance to hold him. It's best, the doctor said when she wailed for her son, and motioned to the nurses to hold Daphne down with a wooden board carved out in the center for her body, *so we don't hurt you, Miss,* one nurse on either side of the restraint as another whisked Hector from her sight, never to be seen or heard again.

This was a common story, Lorena explained to Alex. I have learned so much and it has chilled me to the bone. 250,000 unwed mothers, mostly teenagers like Daphne forced to sign the papers just before giving birth. Some wanted to, most did not. Most of this happened between the 1950s and the 1980s. A quarter of a million babies. A quarter of a million birth mothers. They told the girls they would be taken themselves to an orphanage if they didn't sign and never see their families again. They told them the law required that teenage mothers relinquish their babies. They told them they would go to Hell, whether they believed in Hell or not, if they didn't sign. They told them the baby would hate them forever if they didn't give it up to a proper home with two adult parents who could raise the child right. All through the pregnancy at the home, they pressured the girls to sign, and just about every one of them did. *That's why they invented the restraining board*, Lorena said. *Because they knew it wasn't natural to take a newborn from its mother, they knew it was violent, and they did it anyway.* The *clean-break theory,* the psychologists called it, and so it was: a break, clean through, a rupture to the core.

Fifteen years, the boy become a man. I'd come down to Narooma from Sydney, where I lived, teaching English to migrants and writing fiction at night. I hadn't published a book yet, just some stories in journals, others rejected so many times I just stopped sending them out. My collections weren't displayed yet in bookshop windows, I'd never had a launch, the *Sydney Morning Herald* hadn't yet reviewed me: *a fine debut, a lyrical voice, an eye for the small moments that define our human lives.* Before that, I was anonymous, my writing as much a secret as it turned out my whole life had been, but it was a secret that nourished me, not one that I had to swallow like bad medicine or rotten fruit.

I stopped in at Mason's Fish 'n Chips Shop, where I'd come to pick up a takeaway dinner for Eve and me – a favorite from my girlhood, the family-size special with coleslaw, warm dinner rolls and Mason's home-made lemonade – and there was Alex, ordering the same for him and his uncle. His uncle who was not, it turned out, his uncle. *Not on paper,* is how Alex put it, some nights later, unfurling for me the whole lie, and truth, of his life. If anyone had told me then that I too was a theft and a fabrication, my so-called history like a golden orb's web – elaborate, tensile, entrapping – I would have worried for that person's sanity.

Hector, not Alex. Not given up willingly by his birth mother, Daphne, but stolen.

Naomi, not Nella. Still unknown to me, that Eve was my abductor, not the mother who bore me.

If anyone were reading this, she might think that it is too much of a coincidence that I would marry a man whose secret was so much like my own yet undiscovered one. A bad narrative invention. A plot-turn too many. But Australia is a country in which lost children – vanished, stolen, brought up on lies – are as common as weeds in the garden. In the early days of this colonized land – theft the ground on which the nation was founded. 162,000 exiled convicts, some barely out of childhood, sent across the world forever for stealing a loaf of bread or a neighbor's laying hen. 4,000 Irish Famine orphans driven from their homeland into servitude and worse. Up to 100,000 Aboriginal / Torres Strait Islander children stolen from their families, mostly *half-caste* and raised in white homes, their heritage lost to them as policy, their kidnapping justified by racist laws. And the quarter of a million babies forced into forever-sealed adoptions when their teenage mothers gave birth, the *clean break policy* as brutal as a handkerchief doused in chloroform would be, just before a kidnapper grabs an infant from his knocked-out-cold mother while she rests on a park bench, or lifts the baby from a carriage left in front of the bakery, just for a minute, while her mother runs inside to get loaf of sourdough.

When Alex said the word *stolen,* I remember feeling I'd been burned, as if a human being couldn't bear a truth so fiery. A word like that, spoken of a child, could set a whole bush ablaze, bring down kilometers of ancient eucalypts as if they were kindling.

Another kind of fire overtook us. First, the tiniest flame of attraction, and then the touch of a hand, and then the breath quickening, the bodies leaning into each other, the smell of the other like bush gums stringent and clean and strangely familiar before the bodies burned together into a single new substance: neither ash nor flesh, some ancient alchemical element I can neither name nor ever forget. We believed ourselves transmuted, purified and precious as lead become gold. This is what all lovers believe, and of course it is true, of all lovers as it was for us, for a time. Then the old fixations find form again, you start to look like your old self again, and the gaze of your beloved is a scrutiny hard to bear rather than a blessing.

Imagine running into you in the fish 'n chips shop, he said. *You look just the same, Nella. I knew you right away.*

I knew you right away, too, Alex.

Later I would imagine that we recognized in each other the fact of our abductions. When each of us was taken, did our tiny bodies know the crime and resist? Perhaps in such a child, the shoulders brace a bit or collapse, the muscles around the eyes never quite relax again after the act which startled them so, the back is too taut even when sleeping, and the legs signal running – a shaking foot when seated, a too-fast stride, hamstrings always needing stretching as if the person were a long-distance runner in daily training.

Or perhaps Alex and I emitted a particular odor of sadness only discernible to another who also possesses it, a special pheromone that drew us together. I don't know much about auras, but that is another possibility: some invisible light surrounded each of us, signaling a kinship only those who have been kidnapped wear like a cloak of protection of which they are unaware but can see when another walks into the room.

One of my tribe, such a light may announce. *Family.*

*

We carried those two stolen children into our marriage, your kidnapping known, mine still a secret I did not yet know. The ruptured past like quicksand beneath our feet, even as we thought the ground stable and reliable. You left your flat in Darlinghurst, close to your converted-warehouse art studio, and moved into my Balmain semi. Looking back, I would say our first six months were happy.

We were happy.

Sometimes I find it hard to write about Alex rather than to him. Decades dead, but close to me as the chair he sat in, across the room.

Both of us *loners,* you called us, which had a charge for me that *introverts* softened. We smiled at that, the difference in our dictions, but now I can see that you were signaling a certain pitch of pain I didn't yet know you suffered. An old injury leaving you in chronic distress, as much as if you had broken your leg in a fall, or hurt your spine, or taken a blow to the head in a football game. The bones mend, the bruises fade, but the pain continues for a lifetime, some days sharper than others, but always there as a fixed background hum. Eve used to talk about all her nursing home patients' ailments, how bravely they lived with their day-to-day miseries. You did too, more than I recognized for a time, and then when I did understand your pain, Alex, I was helpless before it.

That rupture for which there is no cure, waiting to be noticed so that it can be known and blessed.

Blessed for bearing witness all those decades to a theft so profound that only acknowledging it brings solace. No other solace but that acknowledgement. Many nights I saw you down on your knees, and though it seemed you were simply levelled by your hurt, I see now you were also bowing, though I doubt you knew that yourself: bowing to the bond with your birth mother who died before you found your way home. Bowing to the rupture for which there is no repair, and to that which can never be torn.

Beauty in blight, blight in beauty: each holds the other in its hand like a seed.

Something in me, too, must have ripped clear through the moment Ruth/Eve took me from my mother in Pittsburgh and fled with me to Sydney. I too must bear the damage of that separation, and the strength of that inseparable union.

Daphne Stavros.

Deborah Gordon.

I bow to them as I write, Alex.

I bear witness.

I say their names.

I write them here in these pages.

What else can I do?

Sometimes Alex would come to my classes. Adult Migrant English Services, Surry Hills branch, right in the heart of the city, a neighborhood just beginning to be gentrified, though in the mid-90s, still a community of working-class families and student renters in small apartment blocks, bed-sitter boarding houses, tiny fibro worker's cottages, moldy brick terraces often broken into units, so that three families might live in a space built for one, or in a terrace house still intact, a group of students might occupy it like bees in a hive. Central Station was an easy walk away for so many for whom cars remained a luxury.

The trees were the aristocrats of Surry Hills, tall and green and flourishing, conferring a kind of privilege over streets where struggle was still the norm: Moreton Bay Figs, spotted gums, plane trees, the springtime purple haze of jacarandas. One of my students told me those trees reminded him of his destroyed homeland and gave him hope that one day the city he had been forced to abandon might recover. He saw the trees as totems, protecting his dream of return. When he walked from his boarding-house room to our classroom building, he said, he talked to the trees all the way.

The building was a gracious brick complex that might have been a Church school once, it had that kind of solid British formality, architectural style imported from the other side of the world, so-called civilization here in the Antipodes, an inviting spaciousness rather than a bureaucratic warren of cubicles, and certainly not a former prison for those early exiled convicts sent by the Crown to colonize Australia.

Alex said he liked to watch me teach. He would sit in the back row, and I imagine some of the students thought him one of their peers, the quiet one who never put up his hand, while some others knew he was my husband likely there, they might have imagined, to monitor me, or guard me from improper advances. A few smiled shyly at his presence, sensing the tender way he watched me.

You don't just teach them English, he'd say. *You teach self-respect.*

He meant the way I had the students interview each other, for example, and write each other's stories as the way they learned the new language into which they all had fallen, as surely as if a boat they all had boarded had turned them out into the sea, where they had to fend for themselves or drown. English was the sea that welcomed them into a new life, and the waters that threatened to overwhelm them at any moment.

Shanifa, from Lebanon, laying her head on the desk one day. A grown woman brought to despair by a grammar that remained daunting after months of study. She tried to muffle her weeping in her hijab, but we all heard her nonetheless. I bent to comfort her, while her classmates averted their eyes, kept themselves busied transcribing the notes they had taken after listening to one another's narratives. *This is why I came, this is where I came from, this is what my life was like at home.* Shanifa, from Burj al-Barajneh, a Palestinian refugee camp in the southern suburbs of Beirut, where her mother and sisters remained while she alone had applied for resettlement. She waited for years. Once in Australia, she planned, she would bring them here, once she was educated, self-sufficient, permanent. She wanted to be a physiotherapist, she told me. She wanted to work with amputees, as her father had been, legless after a fire he might have escaped from as the rest of the family had, if he hadn't run back into their tenement to gather what he could of their belongings: a handful of quilts, a samovar that had been his grandmother's when they had lived in Safed, his daughter Badria's eyeglasses. The ceiling collapsed on him and they brought him out unconscious, without his legs from the knees down. Later, Shanifa's mother would say to her that she prayed he would die in the hospital, so he wouldn't have to face the rest of his life as a cripple. *Then she started hitting herself for having such a terrible thought,* Shanifa said. *I had to hold her hands down, to protect her from herself.* Everything lost in the fire, they were the refugees within a refugee camp, starting over as now Shanifa had chosen to again, in Australia. When she wept in class that day, it wasn't just because of the frustration of the past perfect tense. It was a whole history of displacement, I knew, generations of it, there in her bowed head, her tears, her shoulder that trembled at my touch.

When the students paired off to hear each other's stories, told and written down in English, often someone cried. A listener was overcome by her classmate's ordeal. A teller's memories moved him so, he had to pause, wipe his eyes, blow his nose into the cotton handkerchief he always carried in his pocket.

Hsar from Burma told his story to Duminda from Sri Lanka. *We are Karen people, and the government despises us. In 1997, my father told us again and again, the Burmese Army General Shwe Maung walked on a Karen flag and announced that in twenty years you will only be able to find Karen people in a museum. So my father decided our family must flee. It was just my parents and myself. My sister had died two years before, when the fever took her from us. We were farmers. We walked out of our house that my father had built and left our crops to the five cows and two horses and fifteen chickens. We walked the refugee trail to the border with Thailand and stayed for four years in one of the camps there. Those were very hard days. We lived in tents. Sometimes the water was bad and made us sick. We didn't have much food, and when the rains come, UN couldn't get supplies to us for days. In the mornings, we ate rice, and sometimes that was all we had until the sun rose again. We got thin, we got weak, we cried, we slept. Our dreams exhausted us. My father's heart got sick, and he had to take nine pills a day for the pain. My mother called the camp years* our misery time. *When we were approved for Australia, it was like a nightmare had ended and we were going to heaven. But it wasn't heaven, because my father's heart stopped two weeks after we arrived, even though he did keep taking his pills. My mother says he could not live so far away from our farm. He was planted there, she said. Only there.*

You, too, Alex, torn up from your Stavros roots and given to another family who would never know your true name. Your abduction a wound right through Australia's heart. You and hundreds of thousands of others stolen from mothers, here and abroad, who cried every day, sometimes in silence, for the rest of their lives. Perhaps *after* their lives as well, or so I can imagine.

I began to hear, as if in the far distance, a keening that travels via the wind to every inch of this land. A kind of tinnitus, I thought at first, until I understood it was a mourning song to which my ears had opened. That sound has never left me, and what I couldn't have known until last year is that my own mother's keening, ten thousand miles away in Pittsburgh, was threaded into the wails of all those mothers who cry for their lost children, calling out the names to their last breath and beyond.

I didn't understand then how two lives had come to live in you, Alex and Hector, unreconciled, and the turmoil that created.

We want to be whole, not riven.

We want a single history that runs like a straight road from birth to death, not a sudden detour in which our bearings vanish as surely as stars burning out in the night sky.

We were both stolen from our mothers, this grave fact kept from each of us for decades. The proof of our abductions descended on each of us like a felled tree whose blow we each struggled to survive.

In my case, one deranged woman lifting me out of a hospital bassinet and taking me away to the other side of the world. In yours, two nurses in a South Coast delivery room, holding your mother's body down with a board, doctor's orders, while you were wrested away from her, official policy carried out with the cold efficiency of the Reich, the sounds of her screams melded with your newborn cries. When the Welfare men drove into Aboriginal communities, women all over Australia tried to hide their *half-caste* children in cupboards and under blankets and in the back seats of utes, only to have them stolen from them in front of their eyes, the pleas and the howls of these mothers dismissed as if they were animals penned up on the property and agitated by a stranger's visit in a government car.

And Chana. On the other side of the planet, centuries of Jewish babies murdered and missing. On the orders of kings, princes, Prime Ministers, Fuhrers. *That's your tribe, Nella,* I hear Alex say. *Me, I'm a clean-break sealed-adoption boy. That's my history. My tribe. You haven't claimed yours yet, but you will. Takes time. Lifetimes, I reckon. Lifetimes.*

17

Who knows what accidents are?

When we say, *It was just an accident*, do we really mean *I don't know all the factors that came together at this moment that resulted in this particular event as opposed to the others that might have occurred?*

Why did Ruth Miller steal me instead of another child?

Why did she steal a child at all?

If Chana lived, why wasn't she spared?

Why did Ruth choose Australia as our destination, our exile, our hide-out, our home?

Why did Eve decide to write me her letter of confession?

What did she reveal and what did she fail to reveal, or choose to withhold, or deliberately fabricate?

I don't think *accident* accounts for anything related to my abduction.

And I don't think it explains to me your death, Alex, though all the official documents record the crash as *accident at high speed.*

What kind of *high speed?* Intentional or sleep-induced or alcohol-driven or mechanical failure? And why at that moment, at that rock, at that curve in the road, in the middle of a dark desert night, not even the moon a witness, not even the stars there to offer you direction?

Behind the Balmain semi where you came to live with me from your share-house in Darlinghurst, we converted the garage into a workshop. You created small pieces there, and parts of larger sculptures you completed in your studio in Redfern, a warehouse turned into spaces for artists. You began your work there before you knew you were Hector. A stolen boy yourself, you'd found your way to a workplace in Sydney's Koori neighborhood, the pain of the Stolen Generation, thousands of Aboriginal *half-castes*, they called them, taken by force from their families, many still not accounted for, generations still haunted by the violence and the loss.

Jung says some coincidences are meaningful, and he called them synchronicity.

I have decided that all coincidences are compasses, mirrors, maps, treasure hunt clues.

Who can say how we find our way home, before we even know we are lost?

We married at the Births, Deaths and Marriages Registry in Chippendale, in the city, five minutes from Central Station. An ordinary-looking government office, with a room set aside for weddings, a draped window overlooking a garden of native plants, one wall painted red and spotlights in the ceiling, a sign outside the door that said: *Quiet, Marriage in Progress.* Once inside, across the threshold, we could have been in a great gothic chapel, or the Hyatt Regency ballroom, or a Sydney Harbor boat club looking over the moored yachts of the rich. I wore a short white crepe dress with bold red waratahs printed on the bodice and the skirt, and I carried a bouquet of them, tied with a silver ribbon. You wore your one dressy pair of trousers and a beautiful Nehru shirt we found at the markets – gray silk, with bronze buttons, and embroidery around the stand-up collar. Your parents came, and Lorena, and Eve rode the train up from Narooma, one of the few times I ever knew her to venture anywhere from home.

Afterwards, we all went out to lunch at an Italian restaurant in Surry Hills. We feasted on antipasto, little dishes of gnocchi and ravioli in velvety sauces, broiled salmon fillets and steamed greens, toasted one another with white wine and a bottle of good champagne.

We toasted Daphne, too, the mother from whom you had been stolen.

Your parents turned pale when Lorena offered her tribute: *To my wonderful mother Daphne, who never forgot her Hector, and would have welcomed his Nella into her heart and her home.*

The sealed record, unsealed.

Then dessert: pannacotta with raspberries, and chocolate biscotti with coffee or tea. In the background, Pavarotti sang ballads of longing, adoration, tragic loss and celebration.

Months before the wedding, on a visit to Narooma, we had told Eve about your discovery, that your birth mother had never wanted to surrender you, that she had grieved for you her whole life, that a half-sister had found you and shared with you the truth of your identity. Eve looked frightened, and somehow guilty, as if she had been accused of something herself, rather than entrusted with the knowledge of someone else's awful act, a mother's and a child's unthinkable misfortune. Her raised hands fluttered before her face. *No no no,* she said, as if batting away a swarm of bees. I had thought she meant *I can't bear to hear something so terrible,* but I see now it was her own crime she feared might be disclosed, her decades of disguise threatened by the truth you revealed. There we were, a shudder away from a confession:

> *The police will help. Cases like mine, they are never closed.*
> *In the end, things will be put right. I have nothing more to add.*
> *I hope you can forgive me. I doubt that you will.*
> *Your mother, Eve*

Salt of the earth, you said of your parents, Basil and Thyra Pine. When I met them, Basil was a fit, stocky man, already balding, with a serious face and wire-rimmed glasses that gave him the look of a professor or a dentist, though he'd worked his way up to an auction manager at the Sydney Fish Markets, leaving home at 4 a.m. to be on the floor for the daily sale of seafood. He kept a supply of bright orange vests and white overalls in a bedroom dresser, and *when Alex was little,* he told me, *he liked to dress up in my work clothes and talk in the Greek words for fish I taught him: solomos, garida, barracuda. Because,* I told him, *our people sold fish all the way back in Greece, for generations and generations. Always. We live from the sea. That's who we are.* When your father said *our people,* I heard how he had long forgotten you were adopted. *Adopted* didn't figure for Basil.

You were his son.

You were a Pine.

You belonged to *our people* as if you were blood.

And Thyra raised you like a boy she had carried in her womb, birthed and nursed. I could see it from the way she gazed at you, stroked your head in greeting, made your favorite dishes when we came to visit: Greek potatoes, stuffed grape leaves, her secret-recipe spanakopita, iced tea with mint leaves from the garden. She was a small woman, as Basil was small, but something in her carriage suggested a kind of earthy power, as Greek women often radiate. She wore her black hair in a bun at the nape of her neck, and I imagined that when she undid the band and the hair flowed like a river down her back, she would transform from a plain-looking Marrickville housewife into a woman of great elemental beauty.

Perhaps all of us hide one life inside another, not just those like Eve, for whom masquerade is a furtive part of a criminal life. Perhaps everyone carries a fugitive self behind the decoy of a public one.

When you finally sat down with them and disclosed your meeting with Lorena, the news she brought of your origins, the violence of your abduction in the delivery room, the box of baby clothes she had never surrendered, they wept. Thyra said, *They told us your parents had died in a fire, Alex. They said you were Greek, Alex, like us, and no relatives found in Australia to raise you. We never knew about a Daphne Stavros. We never knew!*

I was there, a witness, that afternoon in Marrickville, the lunch table laden with Thyra's moussaka and Greek salad and honey-drenched baklava. When you asked me to be there that day, Alex, you said *They like you. It will be easier.* For them or for you, I wasn't sure which you meant, but I nodded yes, I would come, for whatever ease I might offer. I could barely imagine how it was for you to have the knowledge you had been given, or how it would be for the Pines to receive. A young mother forced into signing papers of relinquishment, refusing to do so until three days before delivery, and then the way you were wrenched away from her moments after your birth. It seemed then so far from my own circumstances, so remote from my history, however difficult and strange that narrative was. After all, I knew who my mother was, I knew my true name, I knew my history, however scattered its facts.

Or so I believed.

I helped Thyra clear the dining room table, covered with one of her hand-crocheted cloths, and we brought out cups of Greek coffee in Sunday china cups.

I have news, you said, as if you were about to tell them you'd bought a better car, or that we planned to get married – that wouldn't happen for another year – or that you'd sold a sculpture to some rich family in Double Bay, enough to live on for a month or more. News like that. If you had taken a photo of the four of us just then, it would have seemed like a normal Sunday lunch – a hot December afternoon, your dad in his undershirt, your mum fanning herself with the Saturday papers, the African violets on the window-sills wilting, me on the sofa by the open window, trying to position myself in the breeze that came through, and you in the kitchen adding mint leaves to our glasses of ice-water. We would have seemed ordinary and relaxed, rather than four people on the brink of a great explosion about to go off in the center of the house.

I was stolen, not an orphan at all. Stolen right out of my mother's arms. Her name was Daphne Stavros, from Liverpool, and she didn't want me adopted at all. She wanted to raise me herself. Her parents made her give me up. She's dead and they are too, but not my half-sister Lorena, who found me.

Thyra's words came like buckets of water she threw on the burning rug, the furniture about to erupt in flames, the house itself threatened to its very foundations: *We never knew! We never knew! We never knew!*

Basil said nothing. Just shook his head *no no no no*, and refused to look at the photos of Daphne you brought with you, or touch the baby clothes in the box that was yours now. *Because our people sold fish all the way back in Greece, for generations and generations. We live from the sea. That's who we are.*

Had they known the truth back then or not? Had you come to them days after being wrenched away from Daphne – *Hold her down, hold her down* – as the fictional orphan they said they'd believed you were, or as a child stolen from a young girl whose signature on the adoption form could have been forged, for all the genuineness that name attested to? Did they show you that form, and then they made up the story of parents dead in a fire? Or did they know a sixteen-year-old had birthed you and then returned to her family home in Liverpool, bereft and defeated and denied even the right to grieve?

We didn't know, we didn't know, we didn't know.

As for your biological father, Patrick O'Farrell, you traced him to Perth, as far from Sydney as a person can move and still live in Australia. Through the internet, you knew he had married, had three children, divorced, worked at the shipyards, lost his license for driving while drunk, got married again, a widower in his mid-sixties living in a retirement village run by the Church in one of Perth's middle-class neighborhoods not far from the ocean. Three times you thought about flying out to meet him – *Hi there, I'm the boy you said you would ruin my mother over if she didn't get rid of me in one way or another. I'm the one who almost wrecked your life. I might look just like my mother, but your blood flows through my veins, I have the proof, and what are you going to say to that now?* You never went to Perth.

You turned the Balmain garage into a studio, putting up shelves, building a worktable from a salvaged boat deck, hanging industrial lights from the ceiling. And a fold-away bed, *for when I need to lie down and contemplate*, you said. You did your main work in the Redfern warehouse space you shared with three other artists, where the noise of welding, hammering, soldering was absorbed in that former industrial site. In Balmain, you worked on models for the bigger pieces, and sketches for the models. I remember a series of ten watercolors you did, an egret in full flight, the white wings tipped with sun-reflected gold. You pasted them along one wall and they looked like a migrating flock that had somehow detoured from sky to garage and back to sky again.

Trying to catch that freedom, you said, when you brought me in to see the studies. *That bird-grace.*

But it wasn't just your art that took you out there. Sometimes it was rage. A rage of cold silence that came upon you suddenly, or in response to the smallest slight, real or imagined. *So I don't let it out on you, Nella. So I don't do us harm. Sometimes I just need to be alone, you know what I mean?* And as often happens to a partner or child or parent or friend of someone easily angered, I blamed myself for a time, though I think now I always knew the wound was your own. As I knew about Eve, when she turned stiff and silent: *It's not my fault,* a lullaby with which I soothed myself to sleep. *Not my fault, not my fault, not my fault.*

Like Eve, you didn't yell, Alex, you didn't throw things. Your silence would fill the room like a sudden iceberg rising from Antarctica all the way to sub-tropical Sydney. In those moments, the coldness was so palpable, I shivered like a woman caught without a coat in a snowstorm. And the room we were in seemed to grow so large, and you so far away from me in what suddenly seemed like a cavernous space, not our cozy north-facing lounge-room, the sun streaming in through the windows and spilling across the kilim rug, the oak coffee table I picked up from the sidewalk on a neighborhood recycling day, the burgundy sofa. A winter I had never experienced before leached the warmth from the room, from my bones, from my very blood, it seemed. Perhaps in those moments, Alex, my body was remembering my theft from the hospital bassinet, that moment Eve undid my swaddling and lifted me naked except for a diaper into whatever she had devised to wrap me in under her coat on that day that she kidnapped me. And on the far side of the icy chasm, you were the little one wrenched from a teenage mother in a hospital delivery room, after six months in a Home for Unwed Mothers five hours south of Sydney, her own parents never visiting her there once after they left her there, with her suitcase and her stuffed giraffe. *It's for the best, Daphne,* they had told her on the drive down the coast. When it was for the worst.

Who could warm us when those wordless memories rose like ice-water in the veins?

Here is a scene, a fragment, a vignette.

Such writerly words for anguish. Easier to remember the pain through the prism of craft, I suppose. The writer is larger than the sorrow she is remembering. The artist a mother who can hold the bereft child.

We are making supper in the kitchen in Balmain. No cabinets, just lots of open shelving, so the kitchen looks a lot like an art studio, all the supplies and tools visible. Jars filled with whisks and spatulas and wooden spoons, baskets of cutlery, the good knives in a counter-top block, shelves of canisters holding flour, rice, beans, nuts, dried fruit. On one wall, stacks of plates and mugs and various-sized bowls, all different one from the next, all found in thrift stores, a collection I treasure for their glazes and delicate designs and one-of-a-kind uniqueness. *Orphan crockery*, you named them once, your voice both tender and raw.

It is a warm summer night in Sydney, so the windows are open, and the doors ajar to let the breeze through. I am chopping vegetables, you are breading the fish. Reggae on the radio. You make a gin and tonic and I pour some white wine for myself. We are both tired – I have had a long teaching day, and you have been in the Redfern studio since 7 a.m. Cooking together is a way we relax, unwind, move from our separate lives into shared intimate space. I say something like *Alex, hope there's not too much black pepper in that coating,* because you like black pepper a lot and I don't. Do I say it kindly? Does it sound unappreciative? Is it too late in the process to be reminding you of my pepper aversion? I see your body grow rigid. You plop the piece of fish you had been readying for its coating back on to the cutting board, and back away from the counter where you have been cooking. Your hands are raised, as if to ward off attack. *Alex,* I say, the name thrown out like a life-line, though it is unclear to me who needs saving and who might rescue. *Please don't.* You say my words back to me, mockingly – *Please don't, please don't, please don't* – our companionable domestic hour unsalvageable now, the iceberg moves in through the front door and soon we are miles from each other, marooned in the cold, though it is still summer according to the calendar, and the thermometer that hangs outside the kitchen window says 29 C at 6:20 p.m. My eyes are closed, but I hear you slam the back door and your *Fuck this, Nella* like some stranger's curse under his breath, as he passes through the courtyard garden to the converted garage. I'll finish cooking the fish – no pepper I can see in the breading – and steam the vegetables and put the uneaten dinner in the fridge. I'm still shivering. In bed, I wait for you, but you don't return to the house at all that night. You're sleeping alone on the studio foldaway, I'm in our bed, we could be on different continents, that is how immense the loneliness feels, Alex. This is how far it feels you have gone.

In a while – an hour, an evening, a day – your anger would abate and my fear would soften. *It will never happen again,* you would promise me, and though it would happen, again and again and again, I knew you weren't lying to either of us. You believed the rage was spent, or that you could subdue it, and I believed what you believed. Until I no longer could, and you could no longer promise me anything at all. By then you were drinking. By then you were sleeping full-time in the garage. By then our hearts were broken, our minds exhausted, and you decided to move out.

Where are you going?

I'll live in my studio until I figure that out.

Basil and Thyra tried to talk you out of leaving, then begged you to come and stay with them. Lorena said you could move in with her, except that her husband had just been laid off from his job, her three kids didn't even have their own rooms in their small three-bedroom fibro house in Penrith, *and to be perfectly honest,* she said, *I'm scared of your anger and think you should see a counselor, Hector.*

Later, after the accident, she would tell me you said, *I'm not Hector, Lorena. And I'm not Alex either. Who the fuck am I, is what I want to know. Who the fuck am I?*

On the order of service at your funeral, it said you were Alex Pine. Greek Orthodox service in a chapel in Earlwood with burial in Rookwood, Sydney's vast cemetery divided up into sections according to a dozen religions, lawn markers and monuments and wall crypts all arranged in elegant peaceful order, as if a world might exist free of wars and hatreds and genocides, at least for the dead. Basil had bought three plots long ago, when you were a boy, *so we will all be together*, he said, another way he claimed you as kin even in death. I rode with your parents and Eve and Lorena to the chapel and then to Rookwood. It was raining, and thirty of us huddled under black umbrellas around the grave into which your wooden casket was lowered by hand. Some of us sprayed the coffin with droplets of olive oil and wine, threw sprigs of wheat atop your body, and the priest chanted the prayers for the dead: *Sprinkle me with hyssop, and I shall be pure; cleanse me, and I shall be whiter than snow.* Then a handful of sand into the grave: *The earth is the Lord's and the fullness of it, the world and all that dwell in it. You are dust and to dust you shall return.*

Afterwards, we went back to the Pine house, to the table as splendid as any Greek banquet celebration might be, except I did not feel there was anything to celebrate. I did not believe in life everlasting or eternal rest or even the peace that passeth understanding. What could console me? What could offer balm to a heart broken into pieces?

Broken wholly.

Holy broken.

Broken whole.

Ravaged herself, Thyra tried to soothe me. She led me by the hand to their bedroom, rubbed lavender lotion on my pounding forehead, we lay down together on the flowered doona, and she spoke to me in confiding whispers, as if transmitting a secret code. *Now he can have some peace, Nella. He's in heaven for sure. He was a good boy, you know, deep down he was good.* She might have been speaking in a foreign tongue, though her body beside me was a comfort, and I imagined you as a little boy, Alex, right here on this same bed, maybe with a flu or upset by another boy's taunts at school, listening to Thyra's soothing voice, the same lavender lotion on your brow as on mine. My crying quieted, my headache calmed, my heart felt less like a bird intent on breaking out of its cage even if it harmed itself in the effort.

Back in the lounge room, still filled with people come to mourn, I saw Eve crying her own tears. Her second trip from Narooma in four years – first for our wedding, now for your funeral. She had moved away from the others, to the little adjacent sunroom where

Thrya did her sewing. I saw her raise a tissue to her eyes. Eve's back was to the door, but I would recognize that stiff carriage anywhere – my mother's body pulling away from contact, as if all her energy were concentrated on a place within herself, invisible to others, where she could hide in plain sight. It was the body I'd met a thousand times, whenever I asked about our Pittsburgh family, her life before Australia. *Too close, too close, too close*, it signaled, a force field I knew never to penetrate. *Too close.*

And yet she was here to grieve with me. My mother, Eve. Staying a week with me in Balmain. Just blocks from the rooming house to which she had fled, decades before, after stealing me away. Doing my laundry for me, vacuuming, cooking us supper. Scrubbing the tub until it looked brand new, the old claw-footed porcelain's yellow tinge turned factory-white. While Eve cleaned and cooked and cleaned some more, I spent much of the week lying in bed, as if struck down by flu or recovering from emergency surgery. I slept, I read, I meditated. I lived in my pajamas. One day toward the end of the week, I dressed and went out for a walk. I moved slowly, like the convalescent I was, the accident victim whose body will never feel quite right again. It took me half an hour to circle the block. When I returned home, Eve was up on a stepladder in the front room, washing the windows.

This is what a mother does, I thought. Making everything sparkle in a dark time.

When actually she was also intent on scrubbing the record clean, expunging the truth, removing every trace of the evidence: *When you were three days old, I stole you from the newborn nursery in Mercy Hospital and raised you as my own.*

Alex Pine was buried at Rookwood, alongside with 800,000 other souls, a metropolis of the dead, the largest cemetery in the Southern Hemisphere. Elegant green lawns, imposing marble mausoleums, stately burial walls, gardens and paths as beautiful as Buckingham Palace might have: not a dollar spared.

Pine, as *to pine*, the expression of grief, the longing for what has been lost, the yearning that never abates. And conjuring the pine trees brought from the Northern Hemisphere – kidnapped like us, Alex, torn from our roots and transplanted in soil not meant to receive us, though like those pines, becoming what arborists call *naturalized*, just as my students, migrants and refugees, study so hard for their citizenship exam, wear their best clothes for the day they take the Pledge of Commitment at the public ceremony.

In your casket, Thyra put three things: a photo of all of us at our wedding – *that was his happiest day*, she said; a photo of Daphne Stavros as a girl, and the crocheted baby booties from her box of infant clothing. *Because it's right*, Thyra said. *Because she wanted to raise her child and they stole him away from her instead.*

And then the ceremony began.

Ceremony.

That seems like the word to use for the trip I will make to Pittsburgh soon, not a funeral but a naming day, Nella come to claim Naomi, Naomi welcoming Nella home. I've waited more than a year for this journey. *Not ready*, I said to my sister Leah, when we spoke on the phone for the first time in our lives. *Not yet.*

When I woke this morning, Naomi whispered to me, *Now.*

I need more than airline tickets and vacation leave and making sure a neighbor waters the garden in my absence.

What I need is ceremony.

Perhaps that's what I have been creating these weeks here, under Gulaga's gaze. Perhaps I have been writing one long sacred white woman's Dreaming to spirit me from one side of the planet to the other. A star-map of words, songlines on paper, every page a map I am making to guide Nella home.

My name is Nella Pine, and this is my life's story, as new to me as it will be to you who reads it here for the first time.

Alex

I am giving you these words, Nella, it's you who is writing them down.

You can choose the name for what's happening: spirit voice, dreaming, remembrance, love.

It's my voice, that's clear, and you are taking the words down, and for me that's the best any two beings can do.

I wish we had come to this earlier, in the time we had together: each speaks and the other hears it all, says it back.

Call it ceremony.

Call it vow.

Greek.

They said I was born to an unmarried Greek couple who died in a fire, no family members who could raise me, and that was how they got me. Just a baby, they said. That much was the case: I was taken when I was born. Once my half-sister Lorena found me, she gave me the facts which began to come together the way I made my sculptures – the wire, then the clay, then the glaze, and something comes alive and true that wasn't in the world before. You know it in your body, when it comes right.

When I discovered who I was, a boy who would have been Hector Stavros if my mother Daphne had been allowed to raise me, all I never knew rolled out of its sack like stones I didn't know I was carrying. Memories, nightmares, flashbacks – I was pelted asleep and awake by them, and every one hurt, except for the dream I had one night of my birth mother Daphne singing to me in her womb. I was being carried like a baby already born, is how it felt. I could see her and she could see me, even though I was still inside her body. But the carrying was real, and the singing was a lullaby I can still sing, which I do sometimes in the shower, or when I am walking the floors wide awake at 3 a.m. Singing, and carried.

Like I carry you, Nella. Even now, when I am beyond all loss.

Pine, it turns out, isn't their name either. *Pine* in Greek is *Pitys*, and my father's father couldn't see how he could live with that in Australia, all the jokes that would fly at him and his family – *What a pity you got stuck with that name, Mate* or *I pitys you, Pitys, I really do.* So Pine it became, and that's how Dad grew up, and then me after I was adopted. Did they know how Daphne was forced to sign the papers and then held down like a prisoner in the delivery room? What were they told and not told? My parents claimed they never knew I was stolen, but I have seen something flicker through my mother's eyes which tells me maybe otherwise. I didn't battle with her, or my father. They were old. They loved me. They raised me with love. I spared them my fury.

I didn't spare you, Nella, did I?

I raged around our place like you were the one who'd taken me from my mother when I was a baby, then fobbed me off to the Pines, if that is how it happened.

And the so-called birth father, who only wanted me to vanish, in any way possible: abortion (even though he was a Catholic), or adoption, he couldn't have cared what or how. Just to be rid of the baby, and for Daphne to swear to never speak his name.

For a while you were still the wife I loved and trusted. But that changed over the next months. Don't ask me why. Nothing you did or said or failed to do or say. Ghosts took over my soul. Spirits howled. Whatever got ruptured when I was taken from the girl who gave birth to me, that flared up in me like an angry wound that wouldn't heal. Whatever curse Patrick O'Farrell put on her and on me, that too. You became a stranger to my heart. You became my enemy those last mad months. I picked on the smallest things. I went silent. I looked on you with hate. I left our bed. I drove you out, and my heart broke over the loss.

From where I am now, I can finally see how nobody is an enemy, not even the people who came up with *the clean break policy* and the *sealed records rule,* not Daphne's parents who insisted she would have her pregnancy five hours from home, not the nuns there who treated her like a delinquent and me like her crime, not the doctor who delivered me and ordered the nurses to restrain Daphne with the board designed for that purpose, not the welfare worker who got me ready for the next applicants on the list, Basil and Thyra Pine: all of these people whose minds had gone over entirely to the madness they never knew possessed them. I can only say this by having gone mad myself. You cannot see through your thoughts. They form around you like a dense and twisted barbed-wire cage. I should have tried to sculpt that form. Maybe it would have been my way out. But you can't work inside that darkness. Not me. I gave up on clay, worse luck. I left the metal armatures behind. I gave up.

Even when it was good, it was bad, my life. From young. From before I knew. Something in me wobbly, is how it felt. I'd have a good day or more, and then a change would come, just like weather going suddenly from fine to storm. The teachers were always sending me home with a note. *Alex needs to learn to be more cooperative. Alex is not paying attention in class. Alex is a very smart boy, but he doesn't put enough effort into his homework.* Mum would say, *You are sure a handful.* There would be love in her eyes but a worn-out feel in her words. Worn-out love is how it came over to me. Pissed me off. Hurt me. I gave her a hard time, it's true, but not any more than some other boys did their mums. She never hit me, not once. She always made my food and did the washing and sat with me to do my maths at night, and book-reading. Sometimes she wrote my school papers for me, pretty much, just so I would get a decent grade. *Just giving you a little hand up,* is how she put it, but I started to feel it was so she wouldn't be ashamed by my report cards and the disappointment of the teachers. I couldn't see for a long time that she really was trying to help me for *me.* At least some.

Dad, he stayed out of the school thing, the grades. I don't think she ever showed him the notes from the teachers. He wanted me to have a trade, carpentry or plumbing. He couldn't care less if I knew a Banjo Paterson poem by heart like we were forced to learn, or where Mongolia was, or when the First Fleet landed in so-called *terra nullius.*

What changed was Year 7, and my starting to run with some of the older ones, Year 8 and 9. Wogs, the others called us. The ones with English names like Pierce and Simpson and Watson. The ones who used to call me *Whinger, Mouse, Girly.* I was little then, and skinny, and dark. My head still hurts from those words that lodge in the brain like shrapnel. *Whinger Mouse Girly.*

Those older wog boys – Greek, Italian, Lebanese – took me on like a mascot and looked out for me. They liked mischief and worse. I jumped right in. It felt good being with the older ones. It was the best I could figure out as a boy. I was looking for a tribe, I came to see later. A family where I felt I belonged. I didn't know why I didn't feel like that with my parents, with the Pines. Something in me from young, lost from his roots. I was hungering for initiation, deep in my blood where my first memory was hiding. You go after the wrong things when you don't know what the hunger wants, Nella. You go after trouble, and trouble comes to you.

And because of the trouble that found me, I found my way to you. I believe it was inscribed. I have felt that Daphne Stavros guided me. Although it appeared I was sent to Narooma as a kind of punishment for being so *hard to control,* a kind of last-ditch attempt to get me *on the right path*, I believe I was being guided there to meet you, Nella. We were just children the day my uncle took us out to Montague Island, or Barunguba to give it its true name. Children know their kin. You were kin. I knew that right off, on the island.

It was overrun then with kikuyu grass. Bad stuff, strangling the native vegetation like it does. My uncle was an early one for getting rid of it, bringing the earth there back to its true self. The birds know it was bad stuff. They started going elsewhere to nest. The whole place would have been lost to birds if people like my uncle didn't work to bring it back. He worked with the Yuin people on that, worked close with them. He was Greek one hundred percent, but he had this great closeness with the Aboriginal people. Kin don't have to be from blood, I learned. Kin is a heart thing too. Real as genes might ever prove. To Thyra and Basil, I was kin, wasn't I? They were to me too, but it wasn't a clear bond. Too much sorrow in the water, too much heartbreak in the air.

You were such a pretty little girl, Nella. I liked you from the start, and not just because of looks. The way I'd say it now, from this place, is that I saw your soul. It was bright as sunlight in water – how the water itself looks lit from inside and inside and out is nothing but *shine*. I couldn't find my own, sad to say, so I tried to get some of yours. That always turns bad, it's dark with shame, that kind of stealing.

I stole plenty when I was young, but nothing of value. Cigarettes when they were still sold out front, lollies, bags of crisps, a toolbox once from a hardware store, a pair of Nikes on a footpath stand in front of the shoe shop. That kind of stealing. Got caught sometimes, and sometimes didn't. One thing I was always clear about: I felt poorer every time I lifted something. It wasn't that I had no money. My parents were generous enough, and I had part-time jobs from the time I was eleven. What I think is that I was stealing back myself without knowing it: every time I made off with something that wasn't mine, it was like the day I was born and they ripped me away from my mother. Like I was remembering that theft by all the meaningless ones I committed, and somehow that would right the wrong behind them all.

Nella. Nella. Are you getting this all down?

When I saw you again in Mason's Fish 'n Chips, it was like I found myself without needing to steal. That was the feeling. This was clean. This was honest. This was kind. I could feel myself relax into my own skin, which was not a feeling I was used to, or maybe ever had known in my life, except when my mother sang to me in her womb, before I was born and they took me away.

And I gave something precious, too. I would forget that. That I offered as well as received. That I wasn't just another taker, I was good to you in ways I probably don't yet fully remember, but will, having all the time there is now to honor and to mourn.

Your hair was Greek coffee black, your skin ivory against my olive. We both had dark eyes and knew our baby would too. A month before we met in Mason's, I'd learned about my birth, and you were the first person I told. Even before I told my uncle. Because I had been guided to Narooma to meet you, Nella. I am more certain of this now than when I was alive.

What had happened was my younger half-sister Lorena put the clues together, found the proof, searched for me. She used the internet, she found a group who were helping *forced adoptees* find their families, and vice versa. Vanished for twenty-six years, and then turned up alive in Sydney. I saw my face in Lorena's from the moment we met up in a Surry Hill café and she laid out for me the facts of my stolen life. My mother Daphne, the woman who birthed me, was already gone, worst luck. Lorena showed me photos of her. My body recognized her, is how I would say it. I could have crawled up on her lap, left the café and gone right into the photo to be her baby boy again. Her Hector. *Lorena*, I said, *you found some great detective.* They knew know how to get into the sealed files, they know how to interview, they know how to double-check and triple-check what they are told, they know how to follow the clues just like trackers in the bush.

And then, too, I am certain they are guided.

Look up into the night sky, Nella. The routes to home are all laid out, if we learn to read those star-maps.

You're Alex Pine! you said, in Mason's, and I wanted to cry out, *No, I'm Hector Stavros!* And knew right then I'd tell you what had happened to me. Which I did the next day.

We drove out to Glasshouse Rocks, at the south end of the beach. Parked in the cemetery, walked past the graves to the path down to the water. We stopped at Olivia's grave and you left her flowers from the garden. Flowers she would have planted right there at the headstone. From there, we could see the beach below. The ocean blue, the sky blue, the air June-chilled. We walked down the dirt track, not too steep. It's not marked, but we knew it from young. At the white fence, follow the scrub, then over the headland and on down. Most photographed rocks on the south coast, they say. That day we had the beach mostly to ourselves. Us, a few teens skipping school, two young mothers and their babies wrapped up like Eskimos against the cold, one guy with a fancy camera taking lots of photos, one after another. I remember a cattle dog racing back and forth across the sand, chasing an invisible herd.

And the rocks. I didn't take any photos that day, but the details of how they looked imprinted themselves in my mind. Had seen them before, of course, but this day it looked to me like they were lit from inside. 500 million years, they say, those stacked rock towers have been standing there. I saw them first when my parents sent me from Sydney to my uncle. Later, I based many of my sculptures on them. I would say those rocks made me an artist, long before I knew I was one. I loved them for their endurance. Strong but not nasty. How I wanted to be. Especially with you, Nella. Especially.

Time had carved itself into their bodies. They are like trees turned inside out, if the rings were on the outside instead of hidden under bark. Except with the rocks, the rings are zigzag and rough, not evenly round. Stone calendars, back to when we were Gondwanda, one big connected land. Before that, the rocks were under water. And when the land split apart into Africa, South America, Australia,

Antarctica, the Indian subcontinent and the Arabian Peninsula, the Glasshouse Rocks withstood the earth itself splitting apart. Rose up, folded in on themselves, pleating, squeezed by that force like a baby being born. So strong, babies, all the pressure on them and they come through whole. Most do. We come through whole.

When I found out I was *a forced adoption*, my life split apart, again, and I wasn't strong enough to withstand it. A boy-father who had wished me dead, or given away, and his name to never be known *or I will ruin your reputation, Daphne, if I am forced to, I will.* Wherever I stepped, the land gave way. Couldn't hold me steady, is how it felt, though of course anyone watching me wouldn't have known how shaky my footing was. As if other people lived on one earth and I lived on another. Now here you are, the same sinkhole opening under you where solid ground once was.

You'll endure, Nella. Listen well to me. You're glasshouse rock. Diamond-strong.

On the beach that day, I was telling you the deepest secret I hadn't known I had been keeping. What I believe now is that all my troubles from when I was born, and taken, right up to the accident that took my life, came from the secret trying to break through, and me thinking it was poison when it was balm. Inside the hurt, there was the medicine. I had a hint of that, talking to you that winter morning. What you think will destroy you can give you peace. Until then, I hadn't told anyone what Lorena laid out for me that morning at the café. Not my parents, not my uncle, nobody. I had a number to call for counseling, and the DNA tests, but hadn't rung. Kept it inside like I had swallowed a burr, or one coughed up from where it had been stuck for a lifetime. *Hector Stavros.* Maybe the way I screamed when they took me from my mother, or her howl when they pulled me from her arms, ripped something raw in my heart. Big wound, that one. Big damage.

But look, Lorena tried to tell me. *She loved you fiercely. You were so loved.* She showed me the box with the baby clothes in it. Put it right up on the table between us, opened the lid, took out each item and laid it down like it was newly discovered treasure dug up from an archaeological site. Might as well have hit me over the head with a brick. My family were my parents, Basil and Thyra Pine. 147 Challis Avenue in Marrickville, Sydney's inner west. Three-bedroom bungalow. Back garden a small farm of eggplant, tomatoes, onions, beetroot, zucchini, mint, basil. My job to weed it, before I stopped. Greek church on Sundays, before I refused to go.

How do you know it's me? I asked her. *How do you know? They said my parents died in a fire. I was an orphan.*

And yet. When Lorena told me who I was and what had happened to me, inside I felt *Finally.* Some question answered I never knew I had been asking. Some puzzle solved. I knew she was telling me the truth. And when I looked at her eyes, I saw my own looking back. I don't mean *resemblance,* I mean something deeper than that. Soul, spirit, ancestral memory – whatever word fits, I saw that. Not that it made my life easy now. No way. Harder than before. But something at rest. Home. Finally.

You'll see, Nella. You'll see.

I traveled with Lorena to Merimbula, the town on the South Coast where our mother was sent away alone, sixteen years old, pregnant and scared. I didn't tell anyone, not my parents, not my best mates, nobody. I made a reservation on the Virgin flight she already had booked, packed my backpack for a few nights away, and met up in the airport an hour before departure time. I look like Lorena. Clear as day. She had her hair pulled back and was wearing a black hoodie and track pants, same as me. When I saw her from a distance as I walked to the gate, it was like the departure lounge was a giant mirror and when I looked at Lorena, I saw Hector. She was half-Greek like me, though her father was Italian. I didn't get much of Patrick O'Farrell at all, at least not in the looks department. That would have been a sure tip-off, if I had wound up with blue eyes or light hair.

But no, I looked Greek, and so did Lorena. And we looked like the brother and sister we were.

Nothing has felt as strange to me ever as that moment I felt myself approaching myself. Alex reflected to me as Hector, who was actually my half-sister, Lorena. But in that instant, she had stepped aside, it seemed. Stepped aside. So that the man who had been stolen could encounter the man who had been found. I stood still as ancient rock. My mother Daphne sang to me. I knew who I was. I must have looked like I was in a daze or a dream. But I was the clearest that minute I would ever be in my whole life.

Then the airport lounge flooded in again. The voice on the loudspeaker announced the next departure. People rose around me like they had risen from a river. They pulled their suitcases behind them. They were glad to be on land again. Lorena waved. A crowd was lining up at Gate 37. We took our place among them, my sister and me. We showed our boarding passes. We walked through the passenger boarding bridge. A tunnel really, because it was all enclosed. A birth canal, it comes to me now. That's what it was: a birth canal.

Soon we were on board for the short flight, just over an hour. I was two rows back from Lorena. I kept my eyes on her all the way. She had turned back into herself. But I knew she carried Hector in her. Maybe he would show himself again. He did, but always briefly. He would come and go. For years it was like that. Alex Pine looking for Hector Stavros. On the street, in the mirror, running after him in dreams. Chasing a shadow, it felt sometimes. I kept listening for Daphne, but she didn't sing to me again. Or I was too often too drunk to hear her. That moment in the airport, when truth wrapped me in her arms like my mother Daphne would have, if they hadn't held her down with a board, gone. The drinking got bad. What I needed most, I lost. It was like Hector was stolen a second time, worse luck.

In Merimbula, we hired a car and drove out to where the Home had been. Once it had been a convent, then a retreat center for lay Catholics, then the Home which was not at all a home for girls carrying their babies to term. Some came already knowing they would put their infants up for adoption. Others like Daphne were certain they would give birth and then return home with a son or a daughter. Of course, that wouldn't explain, would it, why they were sent away to begin with. If she had reasoned things out, she would have known that Merimbula was a set-up for taking me from her, or else her parents would have kept her with them in Sydney, waiting for my birth and getting ready to help their daughter mother me. But she wouldn't have been thinking clearly at all. Lorena said they told her she could think it all through while she was at the Home, and if she didn't want to go through with an adoption, she needn't. That was a lie, her parents knew. That was why they never visited her, why nobody's parents did: they might crack, they might back down, they might pack up their daughter's things in her suitcase and take her back home with them.

The building was still there but sold off by the Church to a private owner. He had turned it into a hostel for travelers. In the lobby, where Daphne would have stood with her suitcase and her stuffed giraffe, waiting to be shown her room, her children waited for the manager. *This is holy ground,* I thought. *This is as close to her as I will ever be.* I could feel her loneliness and her fear. I could feel her love for me, a three-month-old fetus not even moving yet inside her. Of course, she was going to return home with me, once I was born. She would play along with this adoption thing, if that is what her parents needed. But in the end, she would have her baby and give it a name – Hector or Helene, depending – and take the child home to Sydney. If her parents wouldn't let her live with them, she would find another place to stay. It would work out, because what choice was there? She wanted me. I was her child. The next steps would show themselves to her, when needed.

We asked the manager if Room 23 was available, and it was. I rented it for a night. I was going to stay there by myself, Lorena in a motel across the road. But we both went up the stairs, two flights, to go inside together. Tiny room, just big enough for a single bed, a nightstand, a small pine desk under the window looking out toward the water beyond the next street. Built-in robe, with drawers on one side. Maybe they hung girly pictures on the walls when it was the Home – fairies and kittens and ladies with parasols. Now a framed photo of a lighthouse hung over the bed. A bowl of shells on the desk. I waited for Hector to find me, but he wasn't there. Alex lay down on the nautical-print bedspread. The sky through the window was a clear and startling blue. Lorena was crying. I was nowhere I knew. I was home.

Are you taking this down, Nella? This will help you get through your own return. That's what it is, though neither of us had known we were lost. Stolen away, raised on lies, the truth kept from us as if it were poison instead of mother's milk.

This truth-making, this story-harvest, this prayer, this song.

Call it ceremony, Nella.

Call it vow.

Leah

1

You called. Yesterday. You said, *Hello, Leah, this will be a shock.*

It wasn't.

I've spent my whole life waiting for you to come back, Naomi. I imagined you'd find me on a bus or at the library or in my classroom at school. You'd tap me on the shoulder three times (I dreamed). I would turn around to see you there. You would look serious and grave. *Hello, Leah*, you would say, and on the phone, you did: *Hello, Leah.*

Finally, I could rest.

You called.

As if I'd held my breath for forty-four years, and now I could exhale.

Hello, Leah. What could feel more natural? One sister greeting another. It never occurred to me you wouldn't find us. Others said you were likely dead. Or could never trace your way back to us. I knew they were wrong. How did I know this? How do you know the sun will rise again, after it vanishes at night? There is an order in things. I trusted that.

It was your absence that was the shock. Mom went to the hospital, birthed you, and came home shattered. I was six years old. *Where is our baby? Where is Naomi?* I asked. Dad said I couldn't keep asking. *It will make her very sick,* he said, as if my questions were the cause of her suffering. As if silencing me could take her pain away. Or his. He spoke for her, but as the years went on, I could see that *taking care of Deborah* was Dad's way of keeping the attention away from himself. He could pretend he was coping, while she was *not doing well.* A friend would phone. A neighbor would stop by. A relative would invite us over for Sunday brunch. His reply was always the same: *I'm sorry, but she's not doing well.* In time, I learned all the words that explained how we suffered: *post-traumatic stress disorder, co-dependency, complicated grief.* And of course, your name – *Naomi* – which was also the word of our cure. Dad is dead, Mom has lost her memory, so I'm the only one left to receive the blessing of your return.

It would be a miracle, our mother used to say, imagining how it would be if you came back to us, realizing she didn't believe you would.

She will come back, I'd answer, stroking her hair, wiping away her tears with my fingers.

She would shake her head, as if to say she knew I was saying that to prop her up. But it wasn't like that at all. To me it was a fact, as ordinary as the knowledge that the seasons would turn.

You were born in the spring. Everything was greening after the long Pittsburgh winter. Outside the bedroom I was meant to share with you, the elm tree's branches were soft now with newborn leaves. Robins nested every year in the tree, and I would watch the eggs hatch. That something could break from within, that there was unseen life preparing itself for discovery, and then coming forth through the aperture of its own making: this fascinated me. Maybe the scientist in me was born then, those hours I spent in girlhood observing the tiny ones emerge from darkness into light. Then the mother would feed the babies, placing the food into their wide-opened mouths. Mom would breast-feed you, as she had fed me. We were like the birds in our own human way. That we were hidden before we were born. That we needed a mother to hold us like a second womb. That Nature included us as much as the robins.

In time, I became a biologist, watching cells of living things reproduce. The world I study is invisible to the eye. That's why I could trust you would return long after others had given up hope. Science is a fierce faith, the secret we try to hide, with all our celebration of objectivity and verification. We're mystics at heart, aligned with the ones who talk with angels and ghosts.

I work with fluorescence microscopy. That means I turn the light on the sample to study its light. Certain materials emit visible light when irradiated with another light of a specific wavelength. Light invisible to the eye will manifest, under the right conditions. The previously hidden properties of a cell show themselves. Bacteria once in the dark reveal every detail of their structure. Proteins shine like stars in a black sky. Can you see the faith in that science? I just kept shining my light on your absence, and now you've received it at last.

Light years, we could say. Light years have passed.

On the day you were to come home, I stayed across the street with our neighbor, Mrs. Lundy. We lived on Beacon Street, in an attached row-house, gray brick, each residence set apart by different plantings in the front yard – one had ivy instead of grass, another an island of rose bushes in the middle of the lawn, ours with a giant hydrangea that bloomed each summer with purple blossoms as big as bushes themselves. Across the street, a few bungalows, a Victorian divided into three apartments, a dozen boxy two-story homes each distinguished by a differently colored awning and tidy gardens. The Lundys lived in one of those, their awning was yellow, and in the front yard they planted dozens of tulip bulbs, red and yellow, that were blooming now, along with a border of white crocuses along the concrete walk to the front door.

It was a Saturday. Mrs. Lundy's husband was working at their hardware store. Not many shopkeepers in our Jewish neighborhood worked on Saturday. But Mr. Lundy reasoned it wouldn't be right to shut down because he was a *necessary service*, like a hospital. What if a toilet overflowed and a person didn't have a plunger? What if the power failed and people needed flashlights? Mrs. Lundy had stopped arguing with him long ago. They didn't have children. We on the block who were young became their adopted family. Hers, really. Because he was always at the store. The yellow awning was like a beacon to us. *Cookies here.* I was Mrs. Lundy's favorite.

But though I felt comfortable in her familiar house, I'd wanted to go with Dad to the hospital when it was time for your birth. He said no. He said it would be better if I was *the welcoming committee.* He said that it would be like a party for Mom and the baby if I greeted you both when you arrived. Mrs. Lundy and I would throw confetti in the air when Mom stepped out of the car with you, it was planned, and I still have that bag of colored paper bits I never got to toss.

I kept waiting for the car to pull up. I stationed myself at the living room window and watched the street. Mom would be holding you. I pictured you swaddled in pink blankets just the way I'd wrapped up my doll and carried her around from room to room, pretending you had already been born, though Mom would still be pregnant for months. You were loved all that time you lived in her womb. You were an invisible presence then, cherished and real. After you disappeared, it was that way again. To me, it's a simple thing how we each continued to love you. Others might label that – *have* labelled that – *uncompleted mourning*, as if our ongoing love was pathological. A condition that needed treatment. An emotional illness from which our family suffered. What did they think we should do, these *experts*? Forget you? Erase you from our hearts? Imagine *that* wounding. Imagine *that* unnatural act. Whatever it cost us to keep you close – Mom's ongoing grief, Dad's never-quenched rage at the hospital and police and journalists who failed to protect and then to find you, my faith that sometimes swerved from a steady patience to a longing for signs that turned you more into spectre than sister – I believe it was all worth it. Necessary.

Without our devotion, mad as it might have appeared, you wouldn't have called me. I believe that. Late though it is in our lives: *you called.*

Morning slipped away. Mrs. Lundy made us lunch: tuna fish sandwiches on white bread, I remember, and slices of tomato and a bag of Wise potato chips she split between us. I put chips on my sandwich. It crackled each time I took a bite. She gave me chocolate milk to drink, the ribbon of chocolate syrup spiraling up the inside of the glass. I could describe her kitchen as if I'd been there yesterday. The pink plastic tablecloth made to look like linen. The wallpaper clusters of strawberries patterning the wall. The windowsill over the sink on which philodendron and ivy cuttings took root in a row of water-filled jelly jars. On the maple lamp table beside the brocade sofa in the living room, the phone rang. From the kitchen, I could hear Mrs. Lundy gasp. It sounded like she could be choking on a chip. I ran in, thinking I would pound her on the back. She was chalk white and not choking at all. Her mouth was opened wide, as if a huge scream wanted to come out but didn't, or as if she were screaming in a range not meant for human ears. An animal scream, that might have registered on a dog or an elephant, but there were no dogs or elephants there. The silence was scarier to me than any sound would have been. Something terrible was happening. I thought *I* was the terrible thing, and then I understood: it was the caller who had delivered unendurable news.

I imagined that Mr. Lundy had fallen off a ladder in the hardware store and broken an arm or worse. Maybe he'd hit his head on the counter and now he was dead, the way I'd seen a bird fall out of the nest and land on the ground, more still than anything I had ever seen before. Mrs. Lundy tried to cover over her horror, but it had split her face open. It could not be made right. Dad had not charged her with the job of telling me that my baby sister had vanished, but he had not taken the task from her. I imagine he said something to her such as *Take care of Leah,* and she took that to mean: *Tell her the terrible truth.*

She took me by the hand and sat beside me on the plastic-covered sofa. Her eyes leaked tears. She was sweating under her arms, big blue stains on her housedress, and the sweat smelled rancid. Nothing about the moment was comforting, however much she tried to offer me solace. I was trembling, and the shaking only got worse on Mrs. Lundy's couch.

A bad thing has happened, she said, her voice so low it was as if she were telling me a secret not really meant for my ears. *The baby is... lost.*

When I heard those words, I calmed down. Fear became irritation. Nobody was injured or dead. Only six, I already knew what do you do when something is misplaced. You look for it and then it turns up. You'd put it back in the wrong spot, or somebody else had moved it, or your friend wanted your toy and had taken it home and her mother made her return it the next day.

The police are looking everywhere, she said, and I thought *Of course they are, that's what you do. You look and then you find what's missing.*

I felt I had to comfort Mrs. Lundy, rather than her having to look after me.

Don't worry, I said, stroking her arm the way I would try to console my mother in the years ahead. *Someone will find her.* I thought of how I'd feared my stuffed octopus was gone and found it two days later in the clothes hamper. Or how Mom was always discovering "lost" socks and sweaters underneath my bed. Once she couldn't find her wristwatch and I spotted it later that morning right in the middle of the backyard, and I ran with it into the house like a trophy I'd won or a treasure I'd located in a game she'd planned all along, without my having known it.

Someone will find her, I said again, because Mrs. Lundy still looked like she'd swallowed something poisonous that was making her sicker and sicker. I had no memory of anything in our house having ever been lost that wasn't then found. I had the faith of a child's limited experience. All my evidence led to that optimistic conclusion.

The television was on. Somebody was winning a refrigerator on *Let's Make a Deal*, and the frenzied audience cheered on the stunned woman. She looked as if she might fall to her knees in front of her gift. She reached out and touched the handle of the door, the way you were supposed to touch the Torah in synagogue when they brought it from the ark and paraded it up and down the rows. Faith can be ignited by anything. How hungry we are to believe that our yearnings will be rewarded, our efforts blessed, our losses restored and made whole.

2

We listened to your silence from all sides.

We saw your absence everywhere.

We smelled your disappearance.

Loss is like that, Naomi. It has volume and texture and complexity. Vivid. A prism of so many facets, it's impossible to count them: everywhere we turned, loss reflected itself back to us. Vanished, you were present. Lost, we held you close.

3

When I think of our parents after you were stolen, the images that come to me are still-lifes.

Not of flowers or fruit, but people quiet as objects arranged on a shelf. The vitality that might bring these pictures to life isn't available. I have heard that at the moment of death, the spirit leaves the body. Our parents didn't die. But something of who they were disappeared with you. Their energy flagged. Their visible light dimmed. A whole family swallowed up in shadows. I was looking for invisible light long before I found it in the laboratory. Or, more accurately, our home was my first laboratory, our parents the beloved specimens on which I trained my microscopic gaze. I had the temperament of a scientist early on: observant, patient, devoted, trusting in the unseen, knowing in my bones that the lost shall be found.

If I'm not careful, I will write about them and forget myself. Because during my girlhood, I had to do that: forget myself, so as not to demand from our parents more than they had to give. Perhaps that is another reason the lab has felt so familiar – when I put on a white coat and take my place at the bench, I enter a dream in which I do not figure. A cosmos on the slide. All my attention riveted on a world in which I am absent, just as you have been absent from us.

Sometimes I wonder how my husband, Brian, has lived with a wife part woman, part ghost. Looking back, that is how I see myself. Something of me vanished with you. I thought I was waiting here all these years for your return, Naomi. But it was also my own. Your kidnapper took two children, not one. An infant she named Nella, and an older girl she never knew had followed the newborn to Australia and lived with her sister all these years.

I was a Ph.D. student when I met Brian. On a bulletin board in the campus Student Union, a flyer caught my attention:

Lunchtime Lecture Series
Assistant Professor Brian Solomon
Department of Law
Wednesday, October 15, Noon
Simpson Lecture Hall, Law School
"Forensic Anthropology and the Remains of the Missing in Argentina"

I showed up with the law students, and some from the Latin American Studies program. The questions after Brian's talk and slide show were about international human rights law, forensic methods for maintaining the integrity of exhumed bones, DNA testing as evidence, possible reprisals from the former military junta. Then my question: *How do you prepare the family when you find the bones of their loved one?*

The lecture hall grew quiet as a funeral home. People lowered their heads, as if in prayer. A moment before, they had gazed professionally as attorneys and scientists at slides of skeletons lifted from the earth, reassembled on steel morgue tables, tagged as evidence of wounds and blows.

With great tenderness and compassion, Brian said. *The families have suffered greatly, during their years of waiting. In that way, they are victims, too.*

Yes, I thought, *I know.*

It would take months of conversations in his office, then meals together in restaurants, and finally a night he drove me home because my car was in for repairs and it was too late at night, he said, for me to travel by bus. I still lived on Beacon Street, with our parents. A kind man reached across my ghost-self to the Leah whom he could touch. His arm around my shoulder, he pulled this shy young scientist closer to him. He kissed me on the cheek. I kissed him back on his. We laughed. It was a cold Pittsburgh night and the windows inside frosted by our breath. It made the car a kind of cave. An intimate space. And then the hug that told me I had been found, who didn't know she had been lost.

I have to say I didn't think I would be one to marry. I thought I would live with our parents until they died, and then live on alone, waiting for my sister to join me in our Beacon Street bungalow. Cutting the heads from the hydrangea each season. Raking the elm leaves from the small front lawn. The bigger yard behind the house had been paved over by a former owner and that's where I rode my tricycle, and then my two-wheeler, in circles around and around the concrete. Mother could keep an eye on me there. She always knew where I was. Sometimes another child from the block came over with her bike, or to play Sevensies with me, bouncing the ball in various configurations against the brick wall under the kitchen window.

Mostly, though, I played alone in that cement yard, under our mother's worried gaze.

I wrote *our mother* now, not just to include you, Naomi, but to evoke on the page the sisterly companionship I missed. *Alone* was how I experienced myself.

The child who remained.

The surviving daughter.

The girl whose sister had been stolen away.

I can't say I was lonely as much as solitary. This prepared me for my life in science. When you work in a lab with others, your inner focus is singular, private. Like a nun, I imagine, always turned inward in prayer even as she toils with the other nuns at the tasks for the day, attends the masses morning and afternoon, walks the labyrinth behind the high walls. *Alone*, she chants to herself as she walks. *Alone, alone, alone.*

How did I allow Brian Solomon into that solitude? I see now I didn't. He was willing to sit beside it. He would be a witness to my isolation. I didn't conceive of it as isolation, of course. Because I was always with you, Naomi. Alone, with you. My ghost-Leah kidnapped along with her baby sister. My Beacon Street Leah caring for our parents from the day they came home without you from the hospital. How I kept an ongoing vigil for you. The sister who was lost and would be found. The one who would return one day, which was why I had to live here for the rest of my life, I believed. To receive you. To welcome you with a meal and a readied bed and long hug from the body I kept in reserve for you.

Brian knew all that with his body, and somehow I could yield myself to him without feeling I was abandoning you. Part of me married, part of me remaining with you in your abduction, and part of me still waiting at home in Beacon Street.

You called, you called, you called.

Brian has his own story too. Everyone does, I have come to understand. A friend said to us, *How do you make up for so many lost years?* and Brian said, *You give each other the stories. Those aren't lost.*

When he was ten years old, his mother was hit by a car as it backed out of a space in the supermarket parking lot one late autumn afternoon. It was a rainy day, the driver's rear windshield fogged over. And perhaps she walked into his path, hurrying to the store before the deluge began, because a crack of lightning and a thunderclap signaled a bigger downfall now. The driver said he hadn't even realized he had hit *the woman* until he heard the screaming of others around him and someone blowing his horn. *She leaves behind her husband, Leonard, an accountant, and their two sons, Brian, 10, and Michael, 13, and a sister, Rose, in Buffalo, New York.*

Leaves behind. So you see, Naomi, how Brian recognized himself in me, and what took him to his work on behalf of the vanished, the lost, *los desaparecidos* of Chile, Argentina, Guatemala, Salvador. The ten-year-old boy enlisted in every search, working aside the attorneys and the forensic anthropologists and archaeologists, the coroners, the detectives, the social workers always on hand to support the surviving relatives when the bones are at last identified and claimed. And how the young Brian is always present when a reunion happens between those who lived, given as children to other parents who raised them as their own, not knowing their adopted daughter or son had been stolen away. *For years,* he told me one night, *I waited for our mother to come home, certain that she had been kidnapped and would find her way back to us. I couldn't believe she had died. I waited for her call for years, Leah, until one day I knew it would never come. I wept as I hadn't for the last seven years and made a vow to work for others going through a hell like I had, waiting for a call that never came, or at last hearing that voice on the other end of a phone.*

On the day you called, Brian came home from the seminar he teaches on the International Court of Justice in The Hague. He says he knew what had had happened before I told him. From witnesses he has interviewed, and plaintiffs he has represented, he heard *the lifting of the burden*, he called it. *The end of the vigil.* How the body of such a person relaxes at last. Releases the tension of decades. Breathes deeply for the first time in years, or decades. Brings home the part of herself that has been living in exile, off with the one who was missing.

Writing up the results of an experiment, those would be my conclusions. They were Brian's after years of observations. *The lifting of the burden. The end of the vigil.*

You called.

You are an aunt, Naomi. Our daughter Claire is sixteen years old. She has just learned to drive. Every parent feels fear when their child sets out for the first time behind the wheel of a car. My anxiety runs deeper. That she will be safe in the world has not come easy for me. You can imagine. I have had to stretch myself to live as if I have such trust. Every step toward autonomy has been a joy and a wrench. None more so than her birth.

It took a long time to get pregnant – five years. We had given up hoping, and as often happens, what you surrender will manifest. I carried Claire with joy and terror. The terror came as Mom's grief did: bodily ills I tried to explain in medical terms. The headaches meant I needed new glasses. The rash meant I was suddenly allergic to a soap I'd used for ten years. The palpitations came from too much coffee, or chocolate, or the valerian tea I drank to help me sleep. The dizzy spells signaled one vitamin deficiency or another, or an ear infection that wasn't manifesting pain, or pregnancy itself affecting my balance in ways I read about in medical journals. When Mom said she was worried about my symptoms, I said I was *staying on top of things.* Which was truer than I wanted to acknowledge. All my diagnoses sat on top of the truth: I was so frightened our tragedy would be repeated, that the child I carried would be stolen from us just days after I gave birth.

The fear was like a caul that enveloped baby and mother both. Brian had a map of the world on his office wall, and on this map pins mark the places where governments or insurgencies in the 20th century had intentionally stolen children from parents: barely a continent free of the pins. In dreams, pregnant, I was taken like the pregnant mothers of Argentina, spirited away to some prison in plain sight – a school, a garage, an office building, a motel, a police station – where I would be murdered just after delivering the baby, and the baby would be raised by the torturer and his wife, who was so happy for a child after years of infertility. Many nights I had this nightmare. Sometimes our Jewish trauma surfaced in my sleep: I was a pregnant mother in a death camp, or on the run, or giving birth to a child I had to give away to Christians, so that her life might be spared. Sleeplessness felt preferable to these horror scenes.

And then, in the third trimester of my pregnancy, something unexpected happened. I was in the lab, at work on my experiment. A science lab is a kind of chapel. Everyone bent over their microscopes and slides and computers as if studying sacred texts, the concentration is so serious and focused. You could even say *reverential.* Though of course if you did, you would risk ridicule or the kind of non-responsive silence that is particular to academia. The silence that says, *You are irrelevant. Your work means nothing.* And so we keep our mystical leanings to ourselves, Naomi. We adhere to the secular, and pretend disdain for anything else.

But many of us have what I will call *experiences.* We get a glimpse of the infinite, or a radiance presents itself that defies scientific calculation. A music might overtake us when we are close to completing an experiment. Sometimes a voice seems to whisper an unintelligible message we know holds the key to our hypothesis. I have also smelled something like a rose, right there in the science lab, when my research verifies a hunch I have worked on for weeks or months. That day, as the third trimester began, I can only say I was signaled that Claire's birth would be uncomplicated and that we would be safe from harm. In the hospital on the grounds of the university where I teach, the staff are attuned to abductions. Since the case of *the butterfly baby*, protections have been in place, some visible and others not at all.

The caul that had enveloped us lifted, as if removed by a benevolent practitioner, a kind of midwife I could not see, but whose light filled the room with benevolent care. Was it a religious experience? I don't know, I cannot say.

For three months, Claire would now swim in a womb free of terror, calm and nourishing. Antidote enough, I hoped, to the fear-sea of the first trimesters. Medicine for whatever turmoil she had absorbed.

In the lab, I am researching wound-healing in diabetics at the level of the cell, and florescence allows us to see what had been invisible: how other cells that normally would constellate in a kind of cable around the wound fail to respond, and the wound festers. Perhaps these recollections are the medicine our family's wound needs. The actomyosin cable that protects and heals. It's what I trust in, under the microscope. The invisible reveals itself. The cure shines there in plain illumined sight.

I am going to tell you some stories that have lived in the secret dark. I haven't spoken of them to anyone, not even to Brian or my closest friends. I am going to shine the light of telling on these stories, and they will become visible to you. As if I am putting each on a slide and using fluorescence to bring them into view. And then all the other sense impressions awakening, so that a whole lived experience is available to you.

As if you had been there.

As if you could return to the past from which you were stolen.

As if your vocation's premise is now mine.

You could say that this telling-light is the cure for our pain. I say this as a scientist, not a writer, though writing is what I have turned to in these days since you called. And of course, we do write too. Grant proposals, articles in science journals. After an experiment, there is a format in which we record our work:

Title.

Abstract.

Introduction.

Method.

Discussion.

Reference list.

Appendices.

A careful narrative, that format. Very careful. What's omitted is off the page. Decades of stumbling in the dark. Following hunches. Failing again and again to bring an experiment to fruition. Losing our bearings. Beginning again. This is an account of our off-the-page life, after you were stolen from us.

Title.

The 1968 Abduction of Naomi Gordon, the Impact of Her Disappearance on Her Parents and Sister, and the Curative Potential of Narrative on Their Decades of Grief and Trauma

Abstract.

In a three-week experiment, Leah Gordon, the sister of Naomi Gordon kidnapped days after her birth from Mercy Hospital in Pittsburgh, Pennsylvania, decides to write the story of her family's experience during the five decades between her sister's unsolved abduction and Naomi's call from Australia to say she had learned of the crime and was arranging to travel to Pittsburgh. Each day, Leah records a portion of the remembered years. She does this early in the morning, before leaving for her job as a senior researcher at the University of Pittsburgh, Department of Medicine, Division of Endocrinology and Metabolism. She produces memories, along with a description of her inner world as she recalls it, during the years of Naomi's absence up to the moment she receives her lost sister's phone call fifty years after her disappearance. In the writing of her pages, she explores the possibility that this is a healing act, that the family wounding might find some balm in the expression of her recollected experience. She considers the possibility that writing is a kind of immune response, in which the traumatized soul recovers herself.

Introduction.

Here the reader is referred to Attachment One, which begins with "You were born in the spring," and narrates the day and night the investigator spent with Mrs. Lundy, during which the investigator/narrator learned that

Naomi had been stolen from the newborn nursery at Mercy Hospital, and the years of unresolved grieving began for the Gordon family.

Method.

A gathering of memories, both chronologically and associatively, in order to reconstruct for the abducted sister, Naomi, now in contact with the investigator/narrator/sister Leah, the events and texture of the years of her disappearance, as experienced by her sister and parents, Paul and Deborah Gordon.

Discussion.

(*In progress*)

Reference list.

(*Yet to be constructed*)

Appendices.

(Saved baby clothing, a mobile meant to hang over Naomi's crib, the photo taken in the hospital one hour after her birth, newspaper clippings following the progress of the police investigation into Naomi's abduction, other family memorabilia gathered in the decades following the kidnapping and kept in a cedar "hope chest" for Naomi, in the event she might be found).

When I feel overwhelmed, Naomi, writing down what I recall, I turn to this format from my science life, and it calms me. Yes, I can do this. Yes, I can gather the needed memories. Yes, I can justify the anecdotal approach as sound. My trust in method returns. My training supports me. I can continue.

You give each other the stories. They haven't been lost.

When she was too tired to shop, and I was old enough, Mom would give me a list, and after school I would unfold the portable shopping trolley and set out to do the errands. We lived a block away from Murray Avenue. A stretch of shops, some with apartments upstairs into which the smells below drifted: fresh bread, pizza, bananas, salami, smoked salmon we call *lox,* the barber's pomade, the beauty parlor's permanent wave solution, the roses wrapped in cellophane outside the florist's. In the street, a chorus in English and Yiddish, as if all those voices had practiced their pitch and their parts. Cars and the 68 bus and delivery trucks in a choreographed ballet of traffic. A pumpernickel rye and half a dozen bagels from Silverberg's: a carton of pineapple juice, two sticks of butter, canned salmon and baked beans and corn niblets from Cabin's Grocery; a freshly-killed chicken hanging from a hook in the window of Weiss's Butcher Shop; and from Cohen's Fresh Produce, one head of lettuce and two tomatoes and a cucumber. At the end of Murray, where it intersected with Forbes, a new library had risen like a palace. I would have loved to go in with the other children, but Mom was at home in the darkened bedroom with a wet cloth on her forehead, waiting for the shopping.

By the time I had finished filling the cart with everything on the list, it was as heavy as if it were a stroller and I was pushing. My little sister, I pretended. Naomi. I would talk to you and pretend I could hear you reply. I am not exaggerating. I spoke both parts, my own and yours. Murray Avenue in the late afternoon was always filled with people. No doubt they heard me speaking to the cart. Those who knew who I was might have said at supper, *So sad, she lives in another world sometimes.* Those who didn't know me might have thought me an imaginative child. Felt delighted by my play-acting.

My game was serious, purposeful. Lighting up your invisible light. Finding you in the dark. In that absence into which you had disappeared, three days old, when you were stolen away.

Here we are, Naomi. Home at last.

The day after Mrs. Lundy told me you were lost, our parents came home from Mercy Hospital. *Did they find our baby?* I'd asked Mrs. Lundy when I woke up. She nodded *no.* It was the kind of *no* that had sorrow in it, or fear. The kind of *no* that was like a glass of juice that turned out to be spoiled, and you would feel sick hours after drinking it. Except this *no* illness would last for almost fifty years, each of us sick with your loss in different ways, but all of us stricken. I didn't know how much I still suffered from your absence, Naomi, until you called. Even now I can lapse back into that vague unwellness. I guess that will be true until you arrive here in person.

Antidote, blessing, actomyosin cable regenerated. Soon.

Mom came home in an ambulance, and Dad followed behind in the same blue Ford Falcon in which they had set out to Mercy. The sky was gray, as Pittsburgh skies often were then. Sometimes it could be hard to tell if it was a cloudy day, or if the smoke from the steel mills obscured the brightness that was there. That morning, I was glad for the haze. It felt protective, like a gauze bandage over a wound.

Did they find our baby?

No.

Sunshine would have felt wrong. Not something I knew as thoughts, but something my body knew. I was six. It was overcast, on such a sad and confusing day – that is how I remember it.

I asked Mrs. Lundy why Mom was in the ambulance, and she said, *For extra protection,* and I thought it was kind that the hospital would arrange that for her. That was just before the police arrived in their squad car, just behind Dad's Ford. I saw the guns in their hip holsters. I saw their uniforms, their badges pinned to their chests. One officer took hold of each of Dad's arms. I didn't know if they were offering him support or arresting him. He had turned around to wave to me. He gestured to Mrs. Lundy that she come across the street with me. Inside my little body, feelings crashed and collided. So relieved our parents were home. So frightened to set foot into the house where men in uniforms were taking Mom and Dad.

Mrs. Lundy felt my fear. *Sha, sha, sha, faygaleh,* she murmured to me in Yiddish. Be calm, little bird. And she walked me over the cobblestoned street to our front door, just behind our parents and their captors or protectors, I could not be sure which.

Isn't it strange how everything can change and your house still looks the same? Maybe that was the reason all the familiar details were so vivid to me that day. The table in the entry hall, where my parents put their keys in a small wooden bowl. The mirror over the table, where I could see the top of my head, but not yet the rest of my face. I liked to stand there and jump as high as possible, so that for an instant my whole face appeared in the glass. I think it was a bit like a crystal ball, seeing myself older and taller, suspended there in the timeless air.

The policemen waited on the living room sofa while the ambulance attendants helped Mom into bed. She was wearing the blue maternity pants and the flowered top she'd had on when they had left for the hospital days before. One of the ambulance attendants asked if she would like him to take off her shoes. He asked this very tenderly: *Ma'm, would you like me to remove your shoes for you?* And when she nodded yes, he got down on his knees and untied the laces on her sneakers and took each shoe off as if she were in terrible pain and he was trying to be very careful not to add to it.

Dad and I stood in the doorway, watching. Settled in bed, she held out her arms to me. I can feel her hug to this day. They were her arms, that much was familiar. But they seemed to have changed as well. They felt watery, weak. As if they had lost much of their weight, though they still looked the same. It was like being hugged by a shadow. Then she sank back into the pillow, closed her eyes and fell asleep. Likely she was sedated.

I followed Dad back to the living room, where the officers sat on our paisley-patterned slipcovered sofa. Mom had made the slipcover. She was *good with her hands,* Dad often said. Not a man given to praise, but this was one of Mom's qualities he openly admired. Her sewing, her cooking, her paint-by-numbers landscapes she found frames for at the Salvation Army Store.

We need to collect relevant evidence, one of the officers said.

Dad said, *But she was kidnapped from the hospital.*

We don't know who took her yet, the officer said.

And placing his fingerprint kit on the coffee table.

You don't possibly think – Dad said, and then he sank down into the La-Z-Boy vinyl chair. He didn't say anything else. He surrendered himself. One of the officers dipped Dad's fingers, one by one, into the black dusty medium and pressed them to paper spread out on the mahogany coffee table. Right beside the cut-glass candy dish and the metal coasters stacked up in their holder. The other policeman held open a plastic sleeve into which the paper was placed. I remember thinking this looked like fun, but Dad wasn't enjoying it at all. I remember thinking that Dad must have a rash on his hands, and they were treating him the way Mom rubbed calamine lotion on to my arm when I had a mosquito bite.

When they were finished with him, Dad beckoned me to his lap, but something told me my weight would be more than Dad could bear. And so I sat by myself in the wooden rocker. I watched the officers collecting their *relevant evidence,* they had said. I had no idea what *relevant* meant, or *evidence* for that matter.

But a child knows when suspicion has entered a house.

It is its own invisible dust. It settled everywhere, just like the fingerprint dust would cover every surface as they moved to room to room. Not unlike florescence, it occurs to me here. Making the unseen observable. Bringing to light what has been obscured. In two bags like pillowcases, they carried away the bumper-guards from your empty crib, Dad's bowling bag, Mom's sewing box, my jar of modelling clay and three issues of LIFE Magazine from the table beside the sofa. From the kitchen, they took a cast-iron fry pan, the wooden bread box, some of our stainless steel cutlery and a rolling pin. They took items of clothing, a bath towel that had been draped over the tub days ago, and three Life Magazines from the rack beside the toilet. They wrote up a list of what they were taking and handed it to Dad. *We'll have these back to you in a few weeks,* an officer said. As if he were picking up things to be repaired, rather than examined for criminal intent. Dad shrugged, and began to hoist himself out of the lounger, but the same officer said, *We can let ourselves out, Mr. Gordon*, and they moved toward the front door. Then one turned back, and said, *We think we can tell you we don't think you are involved. It's just routine in cases like this, Mr. Gordon.*

Just routine.

Cases like this.

In time, I lost myself as surely as we lost you.

I might even say *I losted myself,* not because that sounds like a child's speech, but because the way I disappeared was self-willed. Of course, physically I was present, but not with the spontaneity of a happy child. I went dark, you could say. I hid out in plain sight. I may as well have been taken into a witness protection program, given a new name and identity, whisked off to a new city and coached in the arts of *lying low*. The girl I was before you were stolen morphed into another child, this one shy when the other Leah had been outgoing and bubbly.

Sometimes a memory has parts that didn't happen at the same time but come together in the brain as a single event. I don't think that is an error. I think it's how we make patterns of seemingly random moments that are in fact connected, though we don't know it until later, looking back and retrieving. Writing *I losted myself* is like that: the afternoon our parents and I returned to our home, without you with us to put to sleep in that long-prepared crib; the day I returned to school, now a child whose baby sister had vanished into thin air; the night I lay in my bed and received, from some disembodied voice I named *Her,* instructions on how to be the daughter our parents needed now, and how to pretend at school that I wasn't suffering the anguish of a shunned girl.

Not shunned in a way most would notice.

Everyone was polite.

But those who had been my school friends didn't make as much eye contact. Or looked away quickly, when they did. And didn't include me in recess games as they had – I would have to ask to join a round of jump-rope or Red Rover. I would have to insert myself into their games of Jacks on the sidewalk, instead of a place being available for me. Of course, all of that became too difficult, so I simply participated in my exclusion as if it were my choice too. I know they were not being cruel for the sake of cruelty. Your abduction frightened them. That was clear to me without my having the words to name it. I must have carried the odor of our disaster as surely as a skunk releases its unbearable odor on a country road. I pretended to be relieved to be alone. They pretended they didn't notice me.

The years passed.

We all grew older.

You think time will stop, but it doesn't. You are both grateful for and horrified that *life moves on,* as they say, which it does. In a way. Your disappearance was a memory that others could forget. The newspaper accounts ended. Your photo wasn't plastered anymore in shop windows on Murray Avenue, in the post office and bank, in the pediatrician's waiting room. The children could welcome me back as if I had moved away from the neighborhood for a time and then returned. Like Joanie Heller's family, who left for Florida when she was in second grade and came back in the fifth. They'd loved the warm weather, but missed Squirrel Hill, and decided to endure again the blizzards and the smoky air for the sake of old friendships and familiar terrain. Or Bobby Sadowsky, from further down the street, whose father got a job with the Department of Housing and

Urban Development, in Washington D.C., moved the family there when Bobby was in fifth grade and came back when he was entering eighth, buying a house on the same block they had left. *Too much politics in Washington,* his mother said, *and people coming and going all the time.* She'd brought us a pot of chicken vegetable soup as if we were the ones returning rather than her family, and she was coming over to welcome us back.

All our grandparents would be dead by the time you were born.

Mom's parents lived to know me, though both died within the first year of my life. I have no memory of them. I only know what Mom shared, which was very little. Because after you were stolen, Naomi, she forgot herself – *losted* herself – as I did. We turned ghostly. We were less substantial than other people seemed to be. I think now it was too painful for Mom to remember her own parents much, her growing up. All those details she would not accumulate with you. Looking back forced her to look forward, and that was unendurable. And if Mom lost herself, I too faded. Looking into the mirror of Mom's eyes, once you vanished, the reflection I longed to see vanished too. What should have shone turned opaque. What might have dazzled, blurred. The experiments I have created for years, I realize now, efforts to rectify that failure between Mom and me. Her light not enough to bring forth mine. No blame. Who would I blame? It was not out of coldness that she turned away. It was out of grief.

I know this much. Her parents came to America from Minsk, already married in the Minsk Choral Synagogue and expected to stay in the house where our great-grandfather had remained, on Moskovskaya Street, after his wife died of influenza while his son was still a boy. In these early years of the 20th century there, Jews and non-Jews lived together as neighbors, and our grandfather's tailor shop was already doing well, just a few years after he opened it around the corner from the house. But one day either our grandfather or grandmother decided they would move to America, leaving our great-grandfather behind. Who moves across an ocean on the cusp of turning eighty years old? They would abandon the life that was then safe, secure, familiar as herring on pumpernickel bread. It could be they sensed the troubles to come, first when the Bolsheviks turned against the Jews, and then later when the Nazis invaded, established the Minsk Ghetto and carried out the exterminations of 75,000 in the *Aktionen,* November 1941 to June 1942. A dream, a warning from a non-Jewish friend, a palm reading. Who knows? They never said what moved them to make that decision, ride a train from Minsk to Berlin, and then on to Hamburg where they had steerage passage on a ship bound for New York. Like millions of others, the Europe they had grown up in dissolved behind them like so much sea-foam. Whatever grief or longing for home they might come to feel, they would never share that with Mom.

Now, writing this long letter to you, Naomi, I see how we came from a history of loss, an inheritance, a legacy that didn't begin with your disappearance.

I wish you could have known Dad. He died almost ten years ago now, and that's when Mom began *to slip,* as she named it herself. *I'm slipping, Leah.* And she'd reach for the wall or the arm of a chair, as if she were falling, though we knew it was another kind of ground giving way.

Paul Gordon. He was what people would call *an ordinary man*. He went to work every day for forty-two years at Gimbel's Department Store downtown – first in kitchenware, then appliances, then stereos and televisions. He was a year short of retiring when he suffered a fatal heart attack, coming home on the 61 bus. They took him to Mercy, the same hospital where you had been born. Mom phoned me while she waited for the taxi she had called. *It doesn't look good, Leah,* she said through her tears. And then just *Paulie! Paulie! Paulie!*

To our mother, Paulie was life-raft, bearing wall, compass. It's no surprise she faltered when he died. *I'm slipping, Leah. I'm losing my way. I'm going downhill. I'm drowning. I'm sinking. I'm going under.* The diagnosis would be dementia, and subsequently Alzeimer's, but her metaphors say something the medical terms don't. How she had relied on her husband, so wounded himself by your abduction, to keep her going from one day to the next. How his death was a loss of fundamental support that allowed her even the little bit of normal functioning she could rely on. To Mom, he was no *ordinary man*. He was her hero. *Paulie, Paulie, Paulie.* I see now that he was my hero as well, though growing up, I didn't realize how valiant he was. How very brave. I saw his struggles more than his strength.

Only now, writing to you, does he clarify.

These words as florescence.

His light revealed.

He grew up in Homestead, a steel-mill Pittsburgh neighborhood where his parents lived, Jewish refugees who fled pogroms in Grodno, Poland for a settled life in America they never took for granted. They came in the early 1930s, just soon enough. Dad said they met in steerage, on the same ship taking them across the ocean forever. They had grown up three neighborhoods apart, but never knew each other until that voyage. Of the voyage, our paternal grandfather only told one story. He said he saw our grandmother lose her lunchtime bowl of soup during a sudden moment of ocean turbulence. This was the only food she would receive until supper spilled across the wooden planks of the bottom of the roiling boat. How he knew he would have to take care of her, find her another portion, and that if he did that, he would take care of her for the rest of their lives. Of this stranger, he said: *It just came to me, she will be my wife.* And roamed the crowd, asking for a spoon of soup from each person until his own empty bowl was full again and he could present grandmother with the meal she thought was lost.

Grodno passed from Polish hands to Russian ones, and then to the Nazis, who murdered almost every one of the 25,000 Jews of the town. Our Gordon grandparents lost all their family. Transported from the Grodno ghettos to Treblinka and Auschwitz. They never talked to Dad about their lost family – parents, siblings, aunts, uncles, cousins. Strangely, accidentally, our family name became a monument to the Grodno dead. A yahrzeit candle that never goes out. At Ellis Island, our grandfather, Isaac Alinsky, had his name changed to Gordon when he answered *Grodno,* mistakenly, to the clerk's *What is your surname?* Later Isaac would see the error on his papers, but having no idea how to appeal this confusion, he decided to accept his bureaucratic fate.

We became the Gordons then.

We became Americans.

We are the descendants of those who vanished.

We never imagined another one of our family would disappear, here in the land that was meant to put an end to such pain. But you have returned, Naomi. You called. That breaks the curse Dad feared had claimed us again. *Like in the Old Country*, he said once. *Overnight, a person you love is lost to you forever.*

Not forever. You called, you called.

Isaac and Lilian Gordon lived above the shoe store they opened on Eighth Avenue. Who knows where they got money to open a store? Who knows why they chose Homestead? That part of the story has vanished, just like you did, Naomi, three days after your birth. Maybe our grandmother brought every cent her family had in a compartment carved into the sole of her boot. Maybe our grandfather borrowed money from the Catholic landowner whose stables he cleaned. Maybe he promised to pay it back with interest once the American fortune began to accrue.

The stories are gone, irretrievable. And yet I am starting to see how imagination is a medium of discovery, how it pieces together clues, assumptions, similar accounts, and from that mix, a kind of history emerges. Not unlike Brian's work with forensic archaeologists, reconstructing the lives of the disappeared from bones, bits of cloth, a few strands of hair.

Of course, no fortune arrived for our grandparents. They lived from month to month, keeping the neighborhood families – mostly Polish and Lithuanian Catholics – in sneakers, Oxfords, work boots and galoshes. When the steelworkers went out on strike, our grandparents kept their children in shoes they sold below cost. Or donated, if the strike lasted too long. *What can you do? Children don't stop growing.* Dad said *Hearts of gold*, and it was no cliché. That was the school Paul Gordon learned in, as much as the one he went to each morning with the steelworkers' children his parents kept shoed. *Heart of gold,* Mrs. Lundy used to say about Dad. *Heart of gold.*

Except toward the detectives assigned to *the butterfly baby case.* That was you, Naomi, named that because of the iodine stain on your brow.

Dad was unforgiving. *How was it,* he wanted to know, *a baby with a mark on her forehead and a woman whose face is all over the papers can vanish into thin air? How is this possible? How could they get into a taxi, or a train, or an airplane without being detected? This is 1968! This isn't the Dark Ages! Tell me how they could just disappear from the face of the earth. Who isn't doing his job, that's what I want to know! Who bears responsibility? This is our child we are talking about. This is Naomi!*

This is what he would cry out in the shower, the way other men sang *Summertime* or *I've Got You Under My Skin.* I don't think he ever knew we could make out his words. As if the force of the water made it impossible to hear. We heard everything, every morning. As soon as he turned off the shower, he went silent, and when he came out of the bathroom, he was his usual mild and kind self. Mom could manage to make his soft-boiled egg and rye toast, buttered, and a cup of coffee from the stove-top percolator. For me, there was oatmeal, with cinnamon and raisins and the milk warmed up in a saucepan. For herself, a bowl of Special K and a glass of orange juice.

We sat at the table like a normal family, and then Dad took me to school, because our parents wouldn't let me walk on my own until I was in ninth grade.

Dad was still alive when Mom had what we called *the episode.* Twenty years ago now. She has lived without her second-born for thirty years. She has tried it all: *gone on with her life, put the past behind her, learned to live in the present.* This is what the books advise, and the well-meaning friends and relatives, and the two therapists she saw a few times each. *Live for Leah,* they counselled. And later, *Live for your granddaughter Claire.*

And she did try, for decades. To *pull myself together,* as she called her ongoing effort, when others thought she should be *rebuilding your life.* For her that was an impossible goal. For Mom, it was as if an invading virus takes over the immune system and renders one ill against all evidence that the illness is past. Auto-immune, we call it. She often felt that she was *falling apart, coming unglued, unhinged, undone.* Her joints might have been about to snap apart, or the collagen holding her skin intact dissolving, that is how viscerally she felt herself stricken. But she learned to pretend things had eased, the crisis time past, and pleasure possible again. *Pull yourself together, Deborah,* I heard her say hundreds of times, to herself, out loud, over the years. Maybe she was washing the dishes, or in the bathroom taking the pink foam rollers out of her hair, or down on her knees washing the kitchen linoleum until it gleamed. *Pull yourself together, Deborah.* And she would return from her task smiling and calm. Or so it appeared.

Not this day. Not this day in the winter of 1993. I am 33. Brian, my husband, is away at a conference in Boston, where he is giving a paper on the most recent technological advances for examining the DNA of bodies exhumed from mass graves. We have a four-year-old daughter named Claire. Claire, for *light.* We live in Shadyside, a Pittsburgh neighborhood full of university types like us: Leah Gordon Solomon, Ph.D., Department of Medicine, University of

Pittsburgh; Brian Solomon, JD, School of Law, University of Pittsburgh. From our row-house on Howe Street, we can walk to work, or bike to Schenley Park, or be downtown in fifteen minutes on the bus. And from our parents, Naomi, it is a twelve-minute drive, and I make it several times a week. To see how they are. To take Mom out for a milkshake at Isaly's or grocery shopping at Giant Eagle. To drop by with Claire, who brings them some delight in ways you would have, Naomi. A baby to love and protect.

On this day, it's just past 4 p.m., Dad is still at work, and Mom is on her knees, washing the kitchen floor. I've just walked into the house, using my key, announcing myself from the front door. Claire isn't with me. She's at her friend Caroline's house, where her mother said it was fine for her to stay until just after supper, so I could have some time with Mom alone. She has been having headaches again, and Dad is worried. *Talk to her,* he has said to me. *She listens to you the best. She needs a check-up. Maybe it's blood pressure. Maybe she needs pills. Talk to her.*

The bucket overturns, flooding the kitchen. It is one thing too much for her. All the dish towels in the bottom drawer cannot soak up this deluge. The spill happens the moment before I enter the room. I hear her cry out. By the time I enter the kitchen, I see Mom there on the floor, her khaki pants wet from the knees down. It looks as if she has been wading in the ocean. The bucket on its side at her feet could be full of shells she collected when the tide went out. This isn't metaphor. This is her actual confusion.

Are we on vacation? she asks me. *Are we at the beach?*

At first, I think she's joking, that she's amused at her situation, but then I see the look of fear in Mom's eyes.

Mom, I tell her. *Mom. We are right here in your kitchen, and we need to mop up all this water.*

In my voice there must have been a kind of command, and behind that my fear. Is she having a stroke? Is she losing her hard-won sanity at last? Whatever she hears in my voice, it makes her even more frightened. *I don't know where I am, Leah,* she says, looking around at the flooded linoleum, formica table and vinyl-upholstered chairs, the Westinghouse fridge, and old gas stove with the pots stored in the oven, the double sink under the window that looks into the backyard where you never played on the swing set rusting out now, and the small garden where Dad grows beefsteak tomatoes in the summer. On the wall, a clock has been ticking since before you were born. None of this is familiar to Mom that afternoon. She knows me, for which I am grateful. But the rest has dissolved. *Leah, I don't know where I am.*

I'm on the phone, dialing 911. *My mother,* I say. *Please hurry.*

In the few minutes it takes for the ambulance to arrive, sirens which frighten her even more, Mom has asked me a dozen times where we are, what day it is, where Paul is and this: *Is it true Naomi is missing? Is it true she's been stolen?* And when I nod yes, each time, a howl rises from Mom's throat I have never heard before. Even when I put my arms around her to console her, the howl is louder than the sirens come to save her. As if her lungs have been storing up this cry of anguish from the moment you were abducted, Nella, and now at last it is released in its full and awful force.

Is it true? Yes, it is.

At the hospital, the diagnosis becomes clear.

Transient global amnesia.

This is what you will find on the website of the U.S. National Library of Medicine:

> Patients are often described classically with an abrupt onset of severe anterograde amnesia. It is usually accompanied by repetitive questioning. The patient does not have any focal neurological symptoms. Patients remain alert, attentive, and cognition is not impaired. However, they are disoriented to time and place. Attacks usually last for 1–8 h.

> Attacks are often precipitated by a Valsalva maneuver or physical activity including swimming, immersion in cold water, intercourse, acute pain, cerebral angiography, coughing, straining to defecate, heavy lifting, sawing and pumping. Psychological stressors (e.g., arguments) are also well-recognized precipitants.
>
> During the episode, all patients are unable to lay down new memories (verbal and non-verbal), and thus experience profound anterograde amnesia. Retrograde amnesia is often present but is of variable duration, which can range from a few hours up to years. The episodes occur in clear consciousness, patients remain fully communicative and alert throughout, and often carry out complex tasks like driving and playing music. However, they are often agitated or anxious, and may repeat the same questions (mostly relating to orientation) every few minutes.
>
> At the cessation of the attack, there is a rapid and apparently complete return of anterograde memory. On formal testing, minor changes in anterograde memory may persist for months, although this is unlikely to be detected clinically. In contrast, retrograde memory is slower to return to normal, with most recent memories returning last. As patients cannot lay down new memories during the attack, they will never be able to recall the episode itself.

This is just how it was for our mother, Naomi. But it is here I see most clearly the gap between the language of science and the language of narrative: *However, they are often agitated or anxious, and may repeat the same questions (mostly relating to orientation) every few minutes.* This not a good representation of Mom's condition. It is an understatement. Those words leave out the howl. They leave out the raw pain from which the howl rose. They leave out the way her eyes looked like someone else's, as if she had been inhabited by a grief so intense, it changed her DNA on the spot, and the eyes she had been born with forgot their genetic code and new eyes darker and more frightened than I had ever seen, looked into my own and I did not recognize them. You were stolen so soon after birth, it must have felt to Deborah Gordon as if her baby had been ripped from her womb. That crime fueled the howl and altered her eyes. That violation, happening now in our kitchen, again and again and again. *Is it true Naomi is missing? Is it true she has been stolen?*

Now that I am a mother, I know that there are two wombs. There is the one in which the fetus develops and around which medical science builds its model of insemination, gestation, birth. And there is another, invisible, in which a mother shelters her child all their lives. Although it seems as if birth has parted the two bodies, in this invisible womb the mother and child remain symbiotically connected, in a medium much like the unseen light I investigate. In Mom's episode of transient global amnesia, she cried out from both wombs: the one out of which you had been born, and the one from which you had been abducted.

What became clear, even to her in her decades of grief, is that though you were stolen, the womb in which her love continues stretched out as far as your kidnapper took you from us. To the other side of the planet, Naomi, I now know. Australia. And you still as close to her as her breath.

I called an ambulance. I feared she was having a stroke. Or perhaps a brain tumor had been growing for years. One of young attendants who helped lift her on to a stretcher knew. *TGA*, he said, not unkindly, but as casually as if diagnosing a scraped knee. As did the nurses in Emergency, and the technicians doing the scans, and then the Resident confirming: *In about eight hours, she'll be herself again. And with no lasting side-effects. It will go as suddenly as it arrived.*

Just as you did, Naomi. Gone as suddenly as you arrived.

Dad arrived at the hospital just behind the ambulance, which I rode in with Mom. Mercy Hospital, once again. How could they take her to the very place of the nightmare she was continually reliving? But it didn't make things any worse or better. I doubt she knew where she was, three floors below the site of your abduction, decades after the act which was as fresh to her now as if you had just been taken from us. And the doctors were right, she would *come to*, as they said, eight hours to the minute, it seemed, when I had found her there on the kitchen floor.

Paulie! she said. *Leah!* when the affliction resolved. *What am I doing here in this bed? Did I pass out? Was there a fire? Have I had an operation? I don't remember a thing. One minute I am washing the floor and the next minute I am here. How is it possible to lose eight hours? How?*

How is it possible to lose a child? One minute asleep in the newborn nursery, the next minute vanished. How?

This is how.

The woman who took you lived just blocks from us. From our house on Beacon Street, walk a few doors to Murray Avenue, turn left and continue past the blocks of shops – delis, dry cleaners, hardware store, bakeries, Shaare Torah Synagogue, the drugstore on the corner of Forward and Murray, then past Poli's Seafood Restaurant and the ritzy Morrowfield Apartments, up the hill and take the first left around to Alderson Street. A street of three-story dark brown brick buildings. Rentals, then. Ruth Gilbert, a nurse at Mercy Hospital, a single woman, childless, had a modest apartment there. She was at 5836, street level, window boxes with well-tended geraniums. A private person, people said. No record, police said. A good nurse, the hospital said. Mostly she'd worked in the general surgery ward. But in the months before she stole you, she'd moved to obstetrics. By choice, it seems. A transfer she sought out. In a photo the papers published of her, and in the Wanted flyers in the post office, nothing indicated a woman who would commit such a crime.

Not that we know what such a woman looks like.

Not that we have evidence in the facial features that indicates such a possibility.

A dark-haired woman with lovely gray eyes. Round cheeks – not a model's high flaring bones. Beauty of a different sort. A mouth that wasn't smiling but seemed it would be comfortable doing so. No downward creases at the corners, as in one who frowns a lot. Her skin looks clear in the photo. From the way her cardigan is buttoned just so over her shirt, with the collar neatly folded over the sweater, you can see she was a tidy person. The picture was on her nightstand, the police said, and she is sitting on a park bench beside her mother. But the police cut out her mother and distributed the image of Ruth, alone. It was the only photo they found of her in the apartment. We don't know if she destroyed others, or took them with her, or never had any of herself. Perhaps she came from a family in which taking pictures was considered bad luck. Or a too-painful reminder of lost ones of whom no images remained.

Ruthie Gilbert, Dad said as soon as he was shown the photo. I didn't hear him say her name then, but he told this story dozens of times through the years. *I went through school with her. Our mothers knew each other. So that's how I know about the sister. Chana, they had called her. They lost her in Poland. We never knew how. Dead or given away or taken. Her mother never said. And mine never asked. You didn't ask. People told what they told. That was that. You didn't pry. But my mother used to say what a terrible thing to have lost their little girl like that.* And then his silence, as the horrible implication emerged yet again.

Once Mom said, *I don't believe she knew what she was doing. That I cannot believe.*

The police said it was conjecture that the loss of Chana was related to the abduction of Naomi. There was no verifiable evidence for that hypothesis. There was no letter of intent, no witness coming forth to relate a conversation, no diary left behind in her tidy apartment on Alderson Street. Detectives are like scientists in that regard: they look for hard data. They need proof. Even before an arrest and a trial, proof needs to accrue. In a way, their investigations are like my lab experiments: a protocol followed without deviation.

But then there are the other processes that don't appear in the documentation: hunches, intuitions, dreams. When asked how he discovered the theory of relativity, Einstein is reported to have said *I dreamed I was a beam of light traveling through the universe.*

One of the first things my husband Brian told me, when he was describing how police departments all over the world search for the missing: along with the tools commonly considered forensic – the fingerprints, the house searches, the witness interviews, the surveillance camera film, the DNA tests – they employ psychics to help them solve cases.

If they employed one to look for you, Naomi, the effort failed. Ruth Gilbert eluded detection the way fluorescence can fail in the lab. The specimen may fade during exposure, so what you think you have illumined vanishes, or is burned by too much light in a kind of incineration of what you hope to study.

Dad couldn't forgive the police for not being able to find you, but I would come to learn that even the most optimal conditions in a laboratory aren't always enough to produce the result for which we have prepared so well.

It takes tremendous faith to persist.

For faith to persist.

Science is a fierce faith: that's the secret we try to hide, with all our celebration of objectivity and verification. We're mystics at heart, aligned with the ones who talk with angels and ghosts.

You called, Naomi. Almost fifty years later, you called.

Deborah

Here I am, Naomi, here I am.

I am waving to you. I am sending you kisses.

At last I can be with you now without the pain.

From the day you were taken until I crossed beyond recall, all I remembered is the shock of your theft.

I remember carrying you. I carried you low and they say that will be a girl, and it was.

I could not remember giving birth.

I could not remember nursing you those first three days.

Even my life before I conceived you became a length of moth-eaten cloth. Decades gone threadbare. An evening here, a day there, my wedding, Leah's arrival, this relative, that friend. A mind in pieces. What remained crystalline, pure as my soprano-like shriek, was the moment they told me you were gone.

Some days the memory was sharp as a surgical cut without anesthesia. Other days a steady gnawing which wore me down. Sent me to sleep or left me dizzy if I tried to get out and do the shopping or meet your sister Leah at the end of her school day and walk home with her, like other mothers did. Because I wanted so much for her to have the normal mother I was before we lost you. But on just those few blocks, from Colfax Elementary to our house on Beacon Street, the sidewalk would waver, the sky would bear down on me, people looked like they were about to fly. It was hard to keep any kind of balance. To trust I could get home.

I pretended it was migraine. I called it flu, or middle ear infection, or allergies. Heart palpitations, thyroid problems, blood pressure low and high. I went for tests and scans and specialist exams. So many appointments! I took pills to calm me down and others to give me energy. I lost my appetite. I ate too much. I developed rashes, aches, swellings and stiffness. I twitched and trembled. I slept too much in the daytime. Nights, I had insomnia.

Sleepless, I was certain I was back in the hospital, and they had come to my room, yet again, to tell us: *Your baby is gone.*

Your father had to rescue me night after night. *Deborah, Deborah, Deborah.* Rocking me like the baby we had lost. In the next room, Leah pretended not to hear me moaning. I pretended she didn't know.

It would have been easier if the hospital had collapsed and pinned me under the debris. Every bone broken, no air, blinded and deafened and left for dead.

But I wasn't dead.

I was a mother whose baby had been stolen from the newborn nursery at Mercy Hospital, three days after the birth.

After some years, I learned how to pretend I was better. But I was only better at pretending.

Others consider this illness I now have a devastation, but for me, it is the answer to my prayers.

As if I rose up out of rubble and made my way back to a life that is whole. Nobody sees my resurrection. To the others I am frail and confused. Beyond help. Mostly mute or given to utterances that sound like gibberish. When I catch sight of myself in the mirror, a ravaged face looks back at me. But behind that mask which the illness affixes, I bask in gratitude.

If I could speak, Naomi, if I had words, these pages would be my gift to you. As I cannot, these pages are your gift to me.

I called to you and you heard!

On the door to my room in the Home, my name: Deborah Gordon. Written in script, but it's from a factory, made to look personal, but not. The collage someone has made of photos from my eighty-odd years – that was done by hand, but whose I don't know. Probably Leah. Or maybe she gave the photos to a nurse, and a stranger put together this assemblage of my life.

The four-year-old in a starched organdy pinafore which spreads out around me like a great sheer wing.

The smiling ten-year-old with her parents, all of us in bathing suits at Pymatuning Lake, where we stayed in the same cottage every summer for a week in July.

My 12th grade high school photo with a white circle painted around my face, as if I am marked for something as yet unknown, singled out.

Your father and I on our wedding day, in the posed formal dignity of Olympic medal-winners being honored for the feat they have just performed.

A young smiling mother with our new daughter, Leah, her face nuzzled into my neck.

Grown-up Leah and I sitting together years later, on a stone bench outside Phipps Conservatory, smiling for the camera your father would have been holding, as we struggled on with our attempts at normal life after you vanished. Though there was never a day that was normal again.

How ridiculous, posting photos from the past on the doors of those whom they believe remember nothing. Or perhaps the doctors suspect that their diagnosis is faulty, that we patients live now in fact in a wealth of memory, everything lost or hidden or buried under time's collapse returned now, restored, better than new, old movie reels we watch while awake and in our dreams, a private theater to which no one else can be invited.

Your birth was the memory I yearned for most.

As if by remembering it, I could find you, wherever in the world you were.

I tried and tried to find it, but like so much of my life before your kidnapping, it was a futile effort. Those hours reduced to smithereens, all details obliterated. Nothing left but a fine powder of pain. I am now in *advanced decline*, Alzheimer's Stage 6, my address a locked ward on the 9th floor.

And here is the miracle, Naomi: you are born again and again, delivered into my arms a dozen times a day. Inside all the forgetting, the memories I need unfurl like fern fronds on a plant given up for dead. Don't try to understand such a mystery. Just trust that I am waiting for you and will know you when you arrive.

Leah told me you have found us.

She doesn't know I understood, but felt she had to tell me nonetheless. In case. Or, she does know and speaks right through the veils of my affliction. *Naomi called,* she says. *From Australia. She has been in Australia all these years, Mother. She didn't know she'd been stolen. She just learned it. She's going to come to see us.* And then she's weeping, lost for words.

Of *course,* the nurses often find me weeping. *Of course*! Weeping for *joy*. How could I expect them to know this? They live on one side of memory, I on the other. A distance that can't be measured or crossed. As if we were on two planets, light-years apart.

Robley can cross. She is the cleaner who comes every day to vacuum and scrub the toilet bowl. Which I use when someone puts me on it, because I can't get there myself. Diapers, yes. Feedings, too, because I can't hold the spoon steady anymore. But Robley looks into my eyes, into where I am being reassembled even as the rest of me is failing. She looks deeper than the others here do, until she finds me beyond the wreckage of my diagnosis. We look at each other in secret. Secret friends. She is the color of coffee and she sings her words in Dominican-sweetened English. *Yes,* she says and puts her arm around me, *Yes, Miss Deborah, you have a good day today.* And in her eyes I see she is certain that I will. Robley, who is no doctor or geriatric social worker or long-experienced dementia nurse. Robley knows. She can cross. Even if I fail all the tests they give me, even if I cannot say my name, even if they have to spoon the oatmeal into my mouth and wipe my chin with a napkin, even if I am in a diaper, the day will be good. Robley knows.

Just after the last century turned – like a page, like a pancake, like the wind blowing out one storm for another – my parents, Esther and Herman Lapidus, bribed their way from Minsk to Boston.

There I was born.

Bedded down in a washtub, my mother said, that someone had left on the street outside the two-room apartment above Feldman's Bakery given to us rent-free for the first six months by Jewish Relief. Every evening Mrs. Feldman placed the leftovers, which couldn't be sold the next day, in a basket in front of the door to *our palace.* Which is what my mother called it. Our palace. The kitchen brimmed with challah, pumpernickel rolls, cheese danish, apple squares. *Like royalty,* she would say. *We ate like royalty there.*

Growing up, I trusted life. It saved us again and again. I wasn't prepared for anything like your kidnapping, Naomi. If I had been cynical, or full of despair, or fearful of others, maybe I would have found a way to soldier on. Your father did. Being a man who was always on the look-out for danger, your theft was the kind of blow he had been girded for all of his life. Not me. I was blind-sided, crushed, as if evicted by life itself. Where was the palace now? Where was the feast? When you are raised by parents grateful for everything, you are not readied for catastrophe. When you feel protected at every turn, you don't understand a universe that will harm you.

Harm, my parents taught me, was what they fled. Harm was what befell the families they left behind, murdered decades later by Hitler. In America, we were palace-dwellers. Safety wrapped us up in her arms, and who could have imagined she would abandon me like an unwanted child on the side of the road?

But now I am found!

The foundling, found. The mother, daughtered.

Your ear to my heart to your hand to the page.

I wrote stories all the time when I was a girl. Just like you. Secret stories in notebooks from the five-and-dime I hid at the bottom of my underwear drawer. Or thought I hid, because doesn't every mother knows what's inside her child's dresser? But she never said that she found my notebooks, and if she did, I believe she didn't read them. My mother respected privacy, having lost it when she fled from Minsk. I consider my stories secret to this day.

They weren't about our family. Not those sorts of secrets. They were dream-stories, made up worlds: animals who went to school, flowers that talked to each other, people who flew through the air. Somewhere between Boston and my move to Pittsburgh, when I was twenty and newly in love with your father, the notebooks vanished. Maybe I left them on the train. Maybe a porter went through my steamer trunk and took them for his child, who had been sick at home for weeks with a chest cough and fever. Maybe I left them behind in our Boston apartment and my own mother saved them as a surprise for when I had my first child, but she died before Leah arrived and all of her possessions were sold off in a yard sale my sister, Sadie, organized with my broken-hearted blessing.

That was a warning, I see now.

My mother dying before you were born.

I didn't read the signal. After all, she had been a sickly woman. And cancer raced through her like the train I had ridden through the night to the city where your father waited for his bride. I could take so little with me, maybe I left the notebooks in my old room of my old life and sped off, the fantasies of my girlhood surrendered to the unwritten life to come.

I have missed those notebooks all my life.

Now you are the writer of stories, Naomi, including my own. You give me back my words. How, I cannot say. Can you?

Maybe the notebooks made their way across the world, from one yard sale to another, until they wound up in the possession of a young woman who decided to teach for a year in Australia, married there and never came home, and the woman who raised you there, the one who stole you and saved you all at the same time, found them in a charity shop where she was looking for kitchen curtains, maybe, or a side table, or a runner for the hall. And found the notebooks in a picnic hamper which she bought instead, and you have cherished them all your life.

Isn't that a wonderful possibility?

Yes, yes, I am still making up dream-stories.

But write this down, too, so whoever reads it will know that anything is possible. Especially what seems not to be. What good is faith in what's likely? It's the belief in the implausible that matters most. Your sister Leah taught me that. She studies invisible light, you know. She is a scientist. If gravity is meant to be trusted, and the earth's rotation, why not my notebooks migrating across the world to my lost child's hands?

I asked my mother last night if she still had the notebooks. She said she had no idea what I was talking about. She is back in Minsk now, but she visits me here. I don't know how. She is long dead, and the door to my ward is locked from the outside. Maybe she knows the passcode. She must. You will need it when you come to visit. Leah will give it to you. Maybe my mother will be here too. What a sweet reunion!

A child should know what her parents' marriage was like. She should know the soil from which she grows. I am sad your father died before you found us, but I have let Paul know you are coming home at last, and my hope is that he will find a way to be here, just like your grandmother knows the way to the ward. I have let her know he might need her help getting in. That's what families are for.

If anyone reads this, they might try and say you have imagined everything. The kidnapping, your life away from us, your return. And these pages too, which I am telling you breath by breath and you are receiving, sure as resuscitation saved my life three times, twice on the living room floor when Leah was still young, and once in the hospital after I fell and broke my hip, which I think was about ten years ago now, in that old kind of time.

Don't let anyone convince you that this is a fiction, Naomi. Trust me. This is my fourth salvation, and you are my rescuer, the one who knows I am still alive when others have given me up for dead, the one who hears my story when others believe I am mute.

It might look to others that my mind grows more and more blank, like a drought-parched lake in which all former signs of life – the water, the fish, the plants – have vanished and only the cracked mud floor remains. But actually, Naomi, I am awash in a flood of particulars. As if a lost world has surfaced from the bottom, the way shipwrecks turn up centuries later or drowned cities rise from the oblivion to which some catastrophe consigned them. And everything is found to be intact – silver candlesticks, carved oak kitchen chairs, crockery as good as new, children's toys, tortoise-shell hair combs, even brocade-upholstered sofas somehow surviving the ruin. I once read about a swallowed-up town in which, forty years later, all the used cars from a local dealership were brought up by salvagers and sold for parts.

I met your father, Paul, in the housewares department of Gimbel's Department Store, in downtown Pittsburgh, where he worked. This is summer, 1963, just months before John Kennedy's murder in Dallas. I have come to visit my cousins on my vacation – the three Meyer sisters who will never marry and remain together in the house on Hobart Street with their Cantor-father, who has rented the Victorian from the synagogue where he has worked from his early thirties until he dies at eighty-two, never missing a Shabbat or a High Holiday, a bar-mitzvah or a wedding. His wife passed away from tuberculosis when the girls were in their teens. They continued to raise themselves, and good they could, because he had little idea how to care for them, having never been involved in the domestic life of the household his entire life. None of his daughters are musical, or even particularly religious. He waits for sons-in-law who never come, and grandchildren never born. It makes his chanting all the more mournful, and beautiful, as if his gift depended on his grief. Not that I ever heard him. But I can imagine.

I've come to Gimbel's to buy the cousins a gift and get myself some underwear on sale. First the gift, and I decide on a candy dish, because I know they like their sweets, especially chocolates, so I will give them a Whitman's Sampler too, along with the dish. I am looking over the display – some crystal bowls, a square pink china piece with delicate roses painted on each side. I choose the pink china. I'll have it gift-wrapped and buy the box of chocolates right there at the counter, where they are stacked. But there is no one at the check-out, and after waiting what seems like a good ten minutes, but likely less, I go hunting for a clerk. A medium-sized man with a nice head of black hair is arranging goblets on a display table. He has sensitive hands. I will always remember that it seemed to me I had met him before, though of course I hadn't, and then I wondered later if it was because he looked like a movie star, not in the Clark Gable category, your father wasn't handsome like that, but pleasant to look at.

Excuse me, I say, and he gives me a kind smile.

Have you done something wrong? he jokes, and I return his smile, and that's how we begin our life together, which I know we will as I watch how carefully he gift-wraps the candy dish. You can tell a lot about someone from the simplest gestures. You can tell everything, really. I would be safe with him. I would be cared for. We would laugh together. The important things are already clear, just from how his hands fold the paper and affix the tape and tie the ribbon and curl the ends of the bow. Later I will learn that he plays the violin, for a hobby, though his big secret was he had hoped to play professionally, in a Broadway orchestra, first chair: that was his dream. But it never came true. He had to earn a living and found the job at Gimbel's and never left. *I'm in retail,* he would say. *Housewares.*

Sometimes he visits me here with the violin. I sit in the dining room, listening to him, though it doesn't seem like the others are at all interested, or even notice, if you can believe that. He plays show tunes for us, sometimes Yiddish melodies he learned as a boy, and he has some classical pieces too. I listen, but not the others. I hope he isn't offended, having made a special effort to entertain us, when he could just pull a chair up and keep me company while I eat. He is younger than he was when he died at seventy-one. Oh, much much younger! He is thirty-one and you haven't been born yet, or stolen, his heart hasn't broken and his dreams aren't plagued with chases down roads that never end for an abductor he never apprehends. He keeps running after you, bundled in her arms as if you were something precious to her rather than a baby she has ripped from her family, and he can never catch up, never run fast enough, never rescue you. He wakes up breathing hard, as if he has spent those hours in a fruitless chase. That's how your father lived with his grief – nightmares that left him less rested than if he had never gone to sleep at all. In the shower every morning, he yells and curses. Yes, curses! We pretend not to hear him. Then he pretends he is ready for the day, a calm man going off to his job downtown. Retail. Housewares. He lived out the next decades as the one who was coping, while I was the parent who never had her feet on the ground again.

Inside myself, I was always collapsing, Naomi, which began the moment at the hospital when they told me you had been stolen away. I fell down inside myself a dozen times a day. Finally, at last, I'm standing firm. Which you will see when you come for our reunion: I will be waiting here, sturdy as an old tree that's made it through a hurricane, and finally the winds have died now. You will be able to walk straight into my arms and we will hold each other for a long time, and the years of your absence will evaporate, as floodwaters do, at last, after a punishing storm.

I've just told your father that you are arriving soon. He falls to his knees, and cries, his head on my lap. I stroke his beautiful black hair. *Paulie, Paulie, Paulie.* He promises he'll be here, with his violin. If you have some favorite songs you would like him to play, just let us know, Naomi.

It is going to be such a wonderful celebration!

Besides you, I am the only one on Earth who experienced your birth. The only one. Think about that. Your birth is our secret knowledge. That's why not being able to remember it has felt like such a punishment. For years, I racked my brain: Let me remember when my water broke, let me feel the first contractions, let me relive getting in the car and riding to Mercy, let me go through Admissions again and the long hours of labor, and being wheeled to the delivery room, the epidural, the nurse yelling *Push, push!* as if she were at some sports event, and then your head coming through, and then your body – *It's a girl!* – and then, for a moment, you resting on my chest before they would have taken you away to clean you and weigh you and diaper you. Not a single one of these details rose up through the fog of my grief. Then, as memory began to fail and functioning declined, I started to notice a new sort of knowing arising inside me. As if a new organ were available. The brain might be plaque-ridden and lobes reduced and neurons diseased, but here where I am now, some other kind of recall thrives. Your birth has returned to me as if it were a year ago, details so vivid I forget my age, and yours.

May 7, 1968. Time is a trick we play on ourselves, this I now understand.

Where I live now, everything happens at once, there is no remembering and no forgetting. Nothing about this in the medical literature. Nobody returns from late-stage Alzheimer's to the world of Time to testify. I could tell your sister about it, and maybe it would become her new field of research. Except I don't have language now, or none that anyone seems to understand. Even Robley – she knows how to find me, but I don't know if she hears what my silence tells.

But you hear, Naomi. I called and you heard.

My story flowers in you and you give birth to it as if it were a precious life, just as I gave birth to you forty-five years ago, before I moved to the other side of memory where, just now, just this minute, I hear you utter your first beautiful cry. *A daughter*, the nurse says. *You have a beautiful daughter.*

And our lives together begin, again.

About
Joyce Kornblatt

JOYCE KORNBLATT lives and writes in the Blue Mountains. An American-born novelist who moved to Australia in 2003, she is the author of four well-reviewed novels: *Nothing to Do with Love*, *Breaking Bread*, *White Water* and *The Reason for Wings* - which have been published in the U. S., England, France, Denmark and Germany. Her short stories, essays and book reviews have appeared in publications such as *The Atlantic Monthly*, *The New York Times*, *The Washington Post*, *Georgia Review*, *Iowa Review* and *The Sydney Morning Herald*.

For 20 years, she was a Professor of Literature and Creative Writing at the University of Maryland in the U.S. In Australia she has taught and supervised post-graduate writing students, been a tutor at Varuna Writers House, and mentored a number of award-winning Australian writers. For many years, she has offered writing retreats and year-long private workshops in Sydney. Joyce Kornblatt lives in the Blue Mountains, Australia, near Sydney, with her husband, Christopher Ash.